MW01148295

1

Your Free Gift

I wanted to show my appreciation for supporting my work so I've put together a Bonus Chapter for you.

(but don't read it yet!)

Just visit:

http://outerbanks2_freegift.gr8.com

Thanks!
Phoebe T. Eggli

Timber Publishing

SAGE ADVICE TO COVER UP A MURDER!

PHOEBE T. EGGLI

Dedicated to my 'family'.

Not all families are traditional or conventional.

It's my hope that you have 'family' in your life;

and that your life is enriched because of it!

Table of Contents

Chapter 1

Situated just south of Kill Devil Hills, NC, Oregon Inlet served to separate the more bustling northern Outer Banks communities from the small barrier islands. A massive hurricane in 1846 created the inlet - a new body of water between Bodie Island and Pea Island. The "Oregon" a ship trapped in the Pamlico Sound during the storm, witnessed the rift-causing event. Thus, the name. This spot had been well-known for ages as the prime fishing spot for any avid fisherman or woman.

William Hawkins spent what seemed to be his entire life with Johnson Shipping International. Now, at age 62, he finally realized his dream…to fish. Anytime, anywhere. He would no longer be a victim of the white-collar meat-grinder. His wife was none too happy with his abrupt early retirement. Frankly, he no longer cared what she wanted. As far as he was concerned, tonight was the most exciting day of his life. No meetings. No status reports due. No finding new ways to cover up details of dirty deals for Mr. Edward Johnson, Sr. No, today was wide open. Nothing for him to do but breathe in the salt air off the Atlantic Ocean as he repeatedly cast his large surf rod and reel into the waters of Oregon Inlet. William meant to spend as much of his retirement right here with a fishing rod in one hand and a bottle of Coors in the other. Most importantly, he meant to spend as much time away from his nagging wife of 40 years.

As the sun descended over the infamous North Carolina dunes, William unloaded his old light blue '72 Chevrolet C20 truck. He had everything he needed for an entire night's worth of fishing:

- One rod and reel
- Full tackle box with all the essentials for surf fishing
- Cooler full of beer and water bottles, with plenty of bait wedged in
- Italian sub on wheat bread with chips from the local bait and sandwich shop
- Extra jacket if the breeze off the ocean got too chilly
- Loaf of lemon sage bread still wrapped in the decorative paper from the Kill Devil Delicacies bakery to snack on
- Beach chair with cup holder
- Camp lanterns and a large flashlight
- Large fish net
- Cell phone (turned off)

Yes, William was set for his first perfect night as a retiree.

Hours later, as the sun began to rise again over the Atlantic Ocean, Logan slowed his scooter down as it traversed the pavement onto the sandy beach of Oregon Inlet. The place was mostly deserted, except for an ancient looking truck parked further out, closer to the rocks bordering the bridge. The young teen didn't see anyone around though. Whoever owned the truck must be nearby as a ragged beach chair was still embedded in the sand, despite the tide threatening to engulf it.

Before unloading his own fishing gear from the small compartment on the back of the scooter, Logan attempted to rescue the chair before it was washed away by the waves. As he moved the chair back to higher ground, he looked around for the truck's occupant. "It's probably some dude passed out after a night of fishing and drinking," he thought as he approached the Chevy. This spot was known for night fishing, but his aunt never allowed him to fish alone at night. Mostly because she knew it was common for night fisherman to bring plenty of alcohol to keep them company throughout the long hours until dawn. With his aunt's boyfriend working the night shift, Logan had to wait for morning.

As the teenaged boy turned the corner of the truck, he discovered an elderly man lying unconscious in the sand. He ran over to check if the man was okay. Logan noticed the awkward position of the man's body, as if he had fallen from the tailgate of the truck over the side. He kneeled beside the white-haired man and shook him slightly in an attempt to wake him. Unsuccessful, the boy worried that the man was seriously injured or had a heart attack. Intending to attempt CPR, he checked for a pulse and leaned over to listen to his chest for a heartbeat. No pulse, no heartbeat, no breath. The man was already cold to the touch.

In a panic, Logan grabbed a cell phone that was clutched in the dead man's hand. He dialed 911. After he relayed all the information to the 911 operator and waited for the paramedics to arrive, the frightened young man thought back to last summer. To say it had been eventful would be an understatement. At the start of his summer vacation, he discovered the dead body of Mrs. Stevenson in his Aunt Mel's bakery – the Kill Devil Delicacies. It had not taken long to prove his aunt didn't kill the woman, but the event had cast a damper over the start of his summer. The majority of the season had been salvaged once they discovered the real killer. Although he admitted it had added excitement to his vacation, he had hoped that this summer would be less dramatic. Sadly, Logan's summer was about to get much worse.

Chapter 2

Here it was the second day of Logan's summer vacation in Kill Devil Hills, NC with his Aunt Melissa and he already experienced a severe case of déjà vu. Just last summer he and his aunt found the dead body of Mrs. Linda Stevenson in his aunt's bakery, the Kill Devil Delicacies. This year he found Mr. Hawkins lying dead in the sand at his favorite fishing spot, Oregon Inlet. Secretly, Logan hoped this was not a recurring theme for his summer vacations. Just like last year, Logan had been taken to the police precinct for questioning. At least this time he wasn't shoved in the back of a squad car. His aunt's new boyfriend, Detective Jason Payne, drove the boy in his personal pickup truck. Worry etched the cop's face. To discover a dead body once was traumatic enough for anyone, but twice? He knew the kid was tough. Still he hoped the boy was holding up on the inside. On the way back from the inlet, Jason gave the boy his phone to call his aunt who planned to meet them at the precinct. All he could think of was that at least this time it appeared the death was due to natural causes.

When they arrived at the station, Melissa was already there waiting. Jason saw the concern written across her fair features. He remembered last summer clearly as well. He knew all too well how she loved her nephew and fretted over his well-being. Although not her fault at all, she still felt she was to blame for all the drama Logan experienced last summer. There was nothing she could've done to change the events of the past, but seeing the young man still in a state of shock from his latest gruesome discovery broke her heart.

Logan tried to smile to reassure his aunt, but his heart just wasn't in it. It was bad enough to come upon a dead person, but did that person have to be a beloved relative of his summer sweetheart, Emily? She was due to arrive in town the next weekend to visit her grandparents. She would be heartbroken at the death of her grandfather. This certainly was not the way anyone should start off their summer vacation.

Jason offered to take Logan's statement quickly so Melissa could take the poor boy home. His new partner, Cory Bronson, stayed behind at the scene to catalog evidence, if there was anything to find. Jason's hunch was that the old man either slipped in the back of his truck or had a heart attack. A quick skim of the surrounding area before he left with Logan didn't raise any red flags. His first gut reaction was that Mr. Hawkins had passed away doing what he loved best – fishing. Before escorting Logan into an office to take his statement, Jason stopped by the Chief's office to inquire if someone had already been dispatched to inform Mrs. Hawkins of her husband's death. Reassured that the task was being taken care of, Jason led Logan to a nearby conference room. Unlike last year, he could question the boy in an open office instead of a closed interrogation room where his answers were recorded and he was watched through the two-way mirror.

The session was short and to the point. Logan told his story a couple times for the record. He arrived on his scooter just before sunrise to fish at Oregon Inlet. His aunt, Melissa Maples, knew he left the house around 4:50 AM to go fishing. Standing in the doorway, she nodded "yes" to indicate she did see him at that time and that he intended to go fishing. Logan explained he pulled up to the sandy shores of the inlet and saw a dilapidated truck at the far corner near the rocks but didn't see anyone around. He explained about retrieving the beach chair from the surf. Then he walked over to the truck and found Mr. Hawkins face down in the sand. At that point, Logan became freaked out but was able to check for a pulse. There was no pulse and Mr. Hawkins was not breathing. He managed to grab the man's cell phone and call 911. Logan implored the detective to believe he didn't touch anything else from that point on. He simply waited for the paramedics.

Satisfied with the boy's statement, Jason reassured Logan that he believed him. "Most likely, son," he began, "Mr. Hawkins died of natural causes. He was old and not in the best health. I'm sorry you had to be the one to find him though. Let's try to not make it a habit every summer, okay?" The detective's slight attempt at humor at least got a small smile out of the boy. His aunt, on the other hand, stood in the doorway and rolled her eyes. Jason offered to drive them home, but Melissa thought it best they get some fresh air. By walking home, they could talk and perhaps grab some muffins and coffee on the way. She had already called her new bakery assistant, Madeline "Maddie" Vittone, an elderly lady recently retired to Kill Devil Hills from Boston. Retirement hadn't kept her busy enough so Melissa hired her shortly after her last assistant had been arrested last summer. Maddie would take care of things at the bakery while Melissa took care of Logan for the rest of the day.

Back at Oregon Inlet, Detective Bronson and a team of uniformed cops searched the beach for any clues to indicate foul play. Everything had been stuffed in evidence bags. There wasn't a lot to take in – just Mr. Hawkins' fishing gear, snacks, and cell phone.

He saw the opened bread bag from his partner's girlfriend's bakery and half considered snagging it for himself, but thought better of it. He loved her lemon sage bread which was indicated on the label. Instead he zipped it up in a police bag and threw it in the back of the squad car with the rest.

As the tow truck arrived to carry off Mr. Hawkins vehicle to the police impound, the young detective looked around the beach one last time. Everyone on the scene believed Mr. Hawkins had probably died from a heart attack or slipped in the back of his truck. It simply made sense. However, something bothered the astute, ambitious detective. He couldn't figure it out at first. Something just did not seem right to him. Shrugging the feeling off, the young detective turned to leave. Opening the door to his squad car, he caught sight of a dead seagull just a few feet away. Nothing unusual about that. Glancing around again, he noticed another dead seagull over by the rocks. Another dead seagull being carried out to sea by the surf. The tow truck pulled Mr. Hawkins truck away. Hitting a bump as the truck traversed the terrain from sandy beach to asphalt, another dead seagull body flopped out of the back of the truck bed. Scouring the scene one more time, Detective Bronson saw a number of the dead birds littering the inlet. One or two were normal, but more than that raised a red flag. He hailed one of the remaining officers over and ordered them to comb the area for the dead birds and to take them in as evidence. With a confused expression, the man nodded his head and proceeded in his grisly task. That pit in his stomach grew as the detective realized that all was not as simple as it initially appeared. Perhaps Mr. Hawkins had been a victim of foul play after all.

Chapter 3

After an incredibly long day, Jason pulled his truck up to the curb just outside Melissa Maple's quaint cottage. Over the last year it had begun to feel like his second home. The relationship had started rocky, especially since he had to arrest her last summer for the murder of Mrs. Stevenson. He hadn't believed she was guilty, but the evidence had been enough to warrant her arrest. Thankfully, the beautiful baker had not held it against him after she was proven innocent.

The rest of last summer they spent getting to know each other. Melissa was widowed after her husband died in a tragic plane crash so she was shy about starting a relationship. Being divorced, Jason empathized. The two had decided to take small baby steps and simply see where things went. An added bonus was his newfound friendship with Melissa's teenage nephew Logan. The boy had been through a lot last summer, but he was strong and resilient. Jason admired the young man's devotion to his aunt. He enjoyed hanging out with Logan. They spent a lot of time fishing at that same inlet where Mr. Hawkins' body had been discovered. The two even surfed together. Yes, he valued his connection with both aunt and nephew. He sincerely hoped that today's events would not dampen their enjoyment of Logan's summer vacation this year.

Logan answered the door and invited Jason in. Initially, they had planned to go surfing that afternoon, but neither was in the mood after this morning. Melissa was busy in the kitchen preparing a mini-feast. Cooking helped soothe her nerves. Although a brilliant baker, especially of fine artisan breads, cooking regular every-day meals was not her forte. Fancy French cuisine, including escargot or pate, were the rock star menu items of her kitchen. Unfortunately, Logan wouldn't touch the stuff. During the summer she tried to fix him ordinary, traditional meals. Tonight's menu included fried chicken and home fries. However, as evidenced by the rancid burnt smell emanating from the kitchen, her attempt at southern cuisine was a failure. Jason joked to the young man, "Looking like pizza again, huh?" Cracking a smile for the first time that afternoon, he laughed.

"Logan," Melissa called from the kitchen, "Can you open the windows in there? Maybe the deck doors, too?" as smoke spewed from the double oven. Cursing to herself, she managed to extract the offending dish with insulated oven mitts and threw it into the stainless steel sink where the sizzling sound was heard throughout the house.

To get out of the smoke filled house, the three retreated to the back deck. Jason couldn't help but laugh at the exasperated look on Melissa's face. Logan joined in, too. "Aunt Mel, seriously you should stick to baking," Logan stated in between laughter. Throwing her kitchen towel at him, she rolled her big hazel eyes as the hilarity of the situation hit her, too. Just then, a neighbor called out to them to ask if they needed him to call 911 for the fire department. Logan responded, "No thanks, Mr. Menkin! We got it covered. Just Aunt Mel's cooking again."

After the smoke cleared, Jason called for pizza delivery. The trio enjoyed their pepperoni and jalapeno pepper pizza on the deck as they listened to the not-too-distant sound of waves crashing on the beach a few blocks away. After finishing his last slice, they decided to take a stroll on the beach. Walking hand in hand, Melissa and Jason lagged behind Logan who was skipping sea shells along the shore. She turned a concerned face to the tall, handsome detective to ask how the rest of his day had been after the discovery of Mr. Hawkins. "Actually, it has been quite an unusual day," he began. "Everything appears as though he died of natural causes, but my partner's gut instinct made him stir up some trouble." Laughing somewhat, he explained, "Cory bagged and tagged over a dozen dead birds from the scene as evidence."

Confused, Melissa asked the evident question, "Why?" Jason didn't have an answer and didn't think Cory had one either. Something about the birds made the younger detective uneasy so he brought them in. Jason had complained on a number of occasions about the younger man's aggressive, ambitious attitude. He was always making more out of something than was there. Jason was used to it, although it was getting annoying. Just a couple months ago, the young cop had insisted that they should've arrested the underage driver they caught on a routine traffic stop. The driver in question had smelled a bit of alcohol, but Cory wanted to search the vehicle for drugs. The teenage kid was known as a bit of a partier, but considering his mom worked as a drug counselor for the county, Jason hadn't seen anything wrong with just calling the kid's mom and issuing the boy a citation. There had been no reason to "make a mountain out of a molehill".

Jason further explained that Cory was pushing for an autopsy of Mr. Hawkins. Since there was nothing to suggest foul play, they needed permission from Mrs. Hawkins. The distraught widow had been adamantly against it. Without her approval, the young detective still insisted on pursuing the possibility that this was a homicide. Jason admitted the kid had good instincts, but he really thought he was off on this one. They were scheduled to meet with the chief in the morning to figure out how they would write this one up – death by natural causes or possible homicide.

Melissa shuttered at the term "homicide". Last year's events flashed in her mind again. If Mr. Hawkins had been murdered, then Logan would be put under closer scrutiny since he had found the body. It wouldn't help that he had been involved in the murder investigation of Mrs. Stevenson last summer. "Seriously," she thought, "can't we have one normal summer vacation without all the drama?"

Up ahead, Logan had encountered his buddy, Tanner Wiggins. The two were catching up from last summer and making plans to ride the waves early tomorrow. Tanner was the son of the town's coroner. He used his familiar connections to keep himself out of trouble when he snuck beer inside his cooler instead of sodas. Melissa and Jason were aware of the other boy's inclinations, but trusted Logan to not partake in any of Tanner's cooler supplies. Aside from the occasional beer, the boy was a good kid. Despite looking like an extra reject from a "Bill and Ted's Excellent Adventure" movie, he was truly a nice kid with a lot more common sense than most teenagers his age. Jason was well aware of the trouble other kids were getting into these days. His gut told him that Logan was smart enough to avoid that kind of trouble.

As the sun set over the famous North Carolina dunes, Melissa and Jason continued to stroll down the beach. Logan stayed behind with Tanner. "Dude, heard about Mr. Hawkins today!" Tanner began. "You found another dead body, dude! What's up with that? We need to find you another pastime or something." Rolling his eyes at the other boy's beach bum attitude and constant use of the word "dude", Logan explained what transpired that morning. He cringed at the memory.

Tanner half-listened as he watched the incoming waves. He could not decide whether he should tell the younger boy something he found out from his dad about Mr. Hawkins' death. Honestly, he never understood what he could tell others and what he couldn't about his dad's work. The tidbit was intriguing enough that Tanner thought it would at least surprise Logan. "Dude, so everyone thinks the old man croaked from a heart attack or something, right? But my dad said that this crazy cop ordered him to perform autopsies on a bunch of dead birds he found at the scene since the dead dude's wife didn't want an autopsy performed on her hubby. That's weird, right?" Logan agreed wholeheartedly. His smile faded as a sinking feeling hit him in the stomach. He couldn't place a finger on what bothered him, but he knew enough to be wary that maybe things weren't as cut and dry as he wished. If Mr. Hawkins hadn't died of natural causes, that meant he had discovered yet another murder victim.

When Melissa and Jason walked back by the boys, he rejoined them. He remained troubled and silent on the walk back. Not wanting to upset his aunt, he determined to ask Jason about the situation with the dead birds as soon as he could manage to get him alone. The moment came just as Jason was leaving for the night. The older gentleman did not seem surprised by the question at all. Placing his hand on Logan's shoulder, Jason assured the young man that there was nothing to be concerned about. It was just a crazy hunch by his crazy partner. Nothing for them to worry over. Somehow, Logan wasn't comforted.

Chapter 4

The next day Jason walked into the precinct hoping his partner had reconsidered his "gut feeling" and the Hawkins case could be closed. After almost a year with his new partner, he was still surprised every time the younger man tried to turn something simple into a bigger deal. He understood. He was once a young buck in the police department with dreams of being a hero as some cops were portrayed on television and in the movies. Working all these years in a small seaside community didn't lend to lots of action-packed excitement on the job. His work mostly consisted of disorderly conduct complaints (mainly tourists), pickpockets, and an occasional stolen vehicle. Last year had been quite the exception with the murder of Mrs. Stevenson in the Kill Devil Delicacies bakery. That one had been one for the ages. Personally, that was quite enough excitement for this cop. Jason preferred the calm days now.

His hopes were dashed as his partner, Cory, rushed over to him as soon as he walked in the door. "Not a good sign," he thought with an inward cringe. His overzealous partner was in more of a tizzy than usual. The young detective was short in stature but broad-chested with dark blonde hair prematurely thinning, most likely due to overuse of baseball caps throughout his lifetime. Melissa had thought he was handsome when Jason introduced them late last summer. Good thing he wasn't the jealous type. He remembered her saying it was too bad he hadn't come to town a couple years earlier. Maybe her former assistant Britney would have hooked up with a good guy cop instead of a self-centered trust fund baby. That would have saved everyone a lot of trouble.

Cory's blue eyes were blazing as he began telling his partner what he had discovered about the dead birds. Strolling past him to the kitchen to fetch some horrible coffee, Jason took a deep breath for patience. Despite the chief of police's insistence to leave well enough alone, the young man had managed to convince the coroner to perform an autopsy on at least one of the dead seagulls. Jason thought Cory must have promised Mr. Wiggins, the coroner, something of value to get him to go above and beyond his assigned duties. The man wasn't known for his initiative. "What'd that cost ya, partner?" he asked. Jason was right. The young cop had to pony up tickets to an Atlanta Braves game later that summer.

Arriving back at his desk, Cory pulled up a rickety office swivel chair and continued his story. The autopsy revealed that the bird had ingested a chemical poison. Jason began to argue that with all the litter pervading the ocean and shoreline, that wasn't really a major finding. The younger cop interrupted him to explain that the stomach contents of the bird did include some garbage, but what was interesting was that it also contained chunks of bread. Again, Jason didn't think that was anything unusual until Cory broke the last piece of news. The undigested bread appeared to be the same bread Mr. Hawkins had with him along with his fishing supplies – Melissa's lemon sage bread. He planned to request the chief approve autopsies on all the birds to see if they all died from the same poison and if the poison came from the ingested bread. If his hunch was correct, he intended to order an autopsy be conducted on Mr. Hawkins regardless of his wife's wishes.

"Whoa. You wish to go against the wishes of his grieving wife? Seriously? The poor woman is going through enough right now, don't you think?" Jason continued, "There is no indication of foul play and we have no motive why anyone would want Mr. Hawkins dead." Detective Bronson was not to be dissuaded. That feeling in his gut told him he was onto something. Jason was simply afraid his partner's gut was going to stir up a lot of trouble for no real reason.

The conversation was cut short when the chief hollered from his office for them both. They past Peter Andrews, lead legal counsel for Johnson Shipping International, as he exited the chief's office. Jason overlooked the man's presence as being of interest since lawyers were in and out of the chief's office all day long.

Chief James Monroe was a normally cheerful man in his early sixties, but today he was far from smiling. Before the two detectives sat down, he glared at the younger man. "Can someone please explain to me why I have a coroner performing autopsies on birds? Last time I checked, as cops we were concerned about crimes against humans, not animals," he railed. Jason decided to let his partner do the talking. He simply sat back in his chair and listened. As much of a case Detective Bronson could make, Jason could tell the chief wasn't buying it. The more animated the younger detective got as he explained his reasoning, the more annoyed the chief seemed to get. Out of breath, Cory pleaded with his boss to allow him to order autopsies on the other birds, and on Mr. Hawkins.

By the expression on the old man's face, Jason knew it was a losing battle. In the end, Chief Monroe instructed Cory to never order forensic tests, and particularly autopsies, unless approved by himself. He also strongly suggested that Jason talk some sense into the young man and keep a tighter leash on him. The bird autopsy hadn't been performed for free. It was considered a waste of the coroner's time and the department's money. Also, the mayor wasn't too happy to hear about it. If the consensus was that Mr. Hawkins died of natural causes, then so be it. He didn't want to hear of the department overstepping its bounds and harassing innocent citizens, and most importantly voters. Last year's ordeal with the now retired Detective Reynolds going after Mrs. Maples for a murder she didn't commit had not set well with many locals. There had been a brief uproar from the community, but thankfully it had died down after the elder detective apologized.

Officially chastised, Detective Bronson made to leave the room, but not without a warning from the chief to "drop it". "Besides", he informed them, "Mrs. Hawkins claimed her husband's body this morning. He is on his way to the funeral home as we speak to be cremated. Memorial services will be held tomorrow evening at the Main Street Baptist Church, if you would like to offer your condolences." With that, he waved them out of his office.

Later that afternoon, Jason called Melissa to let her know he was running late for their dinner date. His partner had been a handful all day after the scolding he took from the chief. He let her know about the memorial service for Mr. Hawkins as she would want to be there. Mrs. Sophie Hawkins was one of her best customers. Also, Logan would want to be there for the Hawkins' granddaughter, Emily. Thinking of the young girl reminded Jason of how sad his own daughter had been when her paternal grandfather had pass away a couple years ago. Jason made a mental note to call his daughter on the way home after work.

Although surprised at how fast the memorial service was planned, Melissa cleared her schedule for tomorrow afternoon. Everyone would understand if the bakery closed early in honor of Mr. Hawkins. She passed along the information to Logan, so he could call his female friend to see if she needed anything. Normally in the south, folks prepare meals for families in mourning or with loved ones in the hospital. Since Melissa was not really good at cooking, she decided to bake some bread for the family. Knowing Sophie preferred her lemon sage bread over any of her other offerings, she immediately went to work in her kitchen preparing several loaves to deliver the next day.

Chapter 5

Logan and Melissa arrived at the church early the next day. The family was already there greeting guests. The young man ran over to Emily and they hugged tightly. Apparently too tightly as Emily's father, Joseph (a.k.a. Joey) looked on disapprovingly and cleared his throat loudly to get his daughter's attention. Embarrassed, Logan attempted to introduce himself, but was cut off by Emily's mom Katie who gushed, "This must be your young man, Logan. Am I right? My, my. He is as cute as you said, sweetheart." Emily and Logan blushed bright red as Joey's expression turned grimmer. Next to Emily was her older brother, Joey Jr. who was now in college. The young man seemed more bored than sad to be standing in a small church for his grandfather's memorial service. He didn't even pay attention to the guests coming in as he was too busy texting from his phone. Katie tried to apologize for his inattention, but Joey Sr. took that opportunity to smack the phone out of his hands and ordered him to "stop screwing around."

Melissa embraced the elder Mrs. Hawkins who dabbed at tears streaming down her face. She thanked everyone for coming to honor her dear, sweet Willie. Her son gave her a questioning look as she had not referred to his father as "Willie" since their early days of marriage. Piano music started to play in the background as other mourners filed in to pay their respects, including Edward Johnson Sr.'s attorney. Melissa recognized the man as Peter Andrews, the attorney Johnson, Sr. had sent to the police station last summer to help out Britney Williams. He had also worked with an entire team of high-powered lawyers to get Eddie, Jr. out of the manslaughter charges from the incident with Mrs. Stevenson. Funny how when push came to shove, the Johnson family had not attempted to provide help to Eddie's girlfriend, Britney once the truth came out.

Melissa's chain of thought was then interrupted as Logan began to speak in a hushed but heart-felt tone. Logan vowed to Emily to be there for her no matter what and he would catch up with her later after the service. She smiled shyly and squeezed his hand as he moved towards the pews with his aunt.

Melissa sat down beside her dearest friend she'd gained since moving back to Kill Devil Hills a few years ago – Cheryl Lankford. The slim, brunette owned the local soup and salad shop across the street from Melissa's own bakery. Besides being a wonderful friend, Cheryl was one of her best clients as her bakery provided the bread bowls and breadsticks for Cheryl's restaurant. Logan took out his phone to entertain himself until the service started until he saw his friend Tanner enter the church. The two boys chatted while Melissa and Cheryl talked in whispered tones.

Leaning close to Melissa, her friend inquired how Logan was doing since she heard he had been the one to find Mr. Hawkins. "Poor boy," she said, "two summers in a row he finds a dead body. He's not going to want to visit anymore." His aunt sadly agreed that perhaps it was too much for the young man. She called his parents to let them know, but once again they seemed ambivalent to whether he stayed or not. Figuring he would get more attention here with her, she decided he should remain for the rest of the summer.

Melissa asked, "Anyone know why the rush for the memorial service?" Cheryl didn't understand it either. Neither woman had ever heard of someone dying one day and being laid to rest within a couple days. It seemed the entire town was talking about it as well, according to Cheryl who was more of a town gossip than her more reserved friend, Melissa. The two women concurred that it was odd, but thought it even stranger that Mrs. Hawkins had Mr. Hawkins cremated. Being a typical southern town, most deceased persons were buried in family plots behind their respective churches or interred in concrete tombs at the local cemetery. Neither had been to just a memorial service with an urn perched on the small wooden table in front of the pulpit along with a picture of the deceased.

Just a few feet away, Tanner mentioned the same thing to Logan. He thought it especially peculiar since his dad had found poison in one of the dead birds found on the beach along with Mr. Hawkins. "Poison?" Logan asked. He had not heard about the seagulls. Tanner explained about the crazy cop who pestered his dad into performing an autopsy on a dead bird. According to Tanner, there had been several dead seagulls brought in with the dead dude's things for examination. Both boys thought it was weird, but their conversation was cut short when the pastor approached the pulpit to ask everyone to be seated so the service could begin.

Throughout the service Mrs. Hawkins let out several wails of sorrow as her husband was memorialized by the pastor and a touching eulogy was given by their son, Joey. Logan felt horrible as he watched Emily's slender body shake as she cried. He wished he could be with her to offer her comfort, but he was restrained to watch with sadness a few rows back. After a moving rendition of "Amazing Grace" from the church choir, the service ended with the pastor welcoming everyone to congregate in the church recreational building for a potluck lunch organized by the ladies of the church. Mrs. Hawkins picked up the urn with her husband's ashes and carried it with her into the other building.

During the luncheon, Cheryl's husband joined the two women. He had been busy at the office and had been unable to get away in time for the service. Ronnie worked at Johnson Shipping International his entire career. He knew Mr. Hawkins well as they saw each other every day until just the other day when the older man had suddenly announced his retirement, effective immediately. "It's so sad," Ronnie began, "William just retired and had his whole life before him. All he wanted to do was spend the rest of his life fishing and spending time with his grandkids. It's just horrible that he passed away his very first day away from that blasted office."

Cheryl asked her husband, "Why did he retire so suddenly? I remember Sophie squawking about it in my shop after he told her. She was less than thrilled." Ronnie assumed the old man had enough of Johnson's dirty deeds in the business world and longed for a simpler life, like they all did. According to Ronnie, all Mr. Hawkins did for the last thirty plus years was keep the boss man out of the fire. Actually, he was surprised Mr. Johnson accepted his resignation at all. Glancing over at Mr. Andrews, the Johnson's attorney, as he spoke to Mrs. Hawkins at length, Ronnie shook his head. Although the sudden retirement was intriguing, the trio decided the true tragedy was that the sweet man had not been able to realize his dream.

Tanner left Logan with Emily while he went in search of more brownies or cookies in the back kitchen of the church. Rummaging through the plates and platters on the counter, he heard the sound of voices arguing just outside the side door. Intrigued, he decided to check it out. What he heard shocked him. Mrs. Hawkins and her son were bickering rather viciously for a family that just lost a beloved husband and father. Joey lashed out at his mom for rushing everything along after his dad had been found dead. Angry that she had simply accepted his father had died of natural causes, he berated her for not allowing the cops to perform an autopsy at the very least. And that wasn't even the most interesting part of the argument. According to the son, dear dad never wanted to be cremated. The family had a large family plot right behind the church. The son even had a copy of his father's will that was given to him years ago because he didn't trust his wife to follow 'simple' instructions.

Apparently, Mrs. Hawkins wasn't in the least concerned about her son's reaction or the fact that she went completely against her husband's last wishes. She stood there stoically clinging to the urn as she sternly told him she did what was best.

Tanner couldn't wait to get back to Logan to relay this sweet, tantalizing bit of information. In his hurry, he knocked over a cheese and crackers platter. Alerted by the noise, Mrs. Hawkins quickly pushed the door fully open. Luckily, Tanner was too fast. He avoided being caught eavesdropping by ducking behind another counter and crawling out an open door to the main room before Joey or his mom even saw his shadow.

Chapter 6

Tanner contained his excitement for the remainder of the afternoon so as to not alert the widow and her son that he had overheard their private conversation. He couldn't make heads nor tails of it though. Why would Mrs. Hawkins purposefully go against her husband's final wishes? The boy didn't really care, but it sure made for interesting gossip. As soon as he saw his buddy Logan leaving with his aunt, the young man followed them out with the excuse that Logan promised to hang with him that afternoon. Confused, the other boy played along. He would rather spend time with Emily, especially after seeing her so distraught today. However, he realized she would be busy with family and friends and he certainly could use the distraction of riding the waves.

It wasn't until the sun was setting over the Atlantic Ocean that Tanner remembered he had something to tell his friend. He fished a soda out of the cooler as the boys rested on a splintered picnic table just outside The Surf Shack. "Dude, you are NOT going to believe what I heard today," Tanner began. He proceeded to tell him about the argument between the widow and her son. Initially, Logan thought it strange but nothing alarming. Then he remembered the other news about the bird being killed by poison. Maybe he was watching too many of his aunt's favorite television crime dramas but it sounded like a mystery to him. Logan decided to talk to Aunt Mel, and maybe even Jason, later that evening about it.

Over dinner – Chinese food that Jason picked up on the way over – Logan broached the subject of Mr. Hawkins memorial service. Jason had been unable to attend due to work commitments, so he was interested in what transpired at the service. Melissa filled him in on how everyone thought it strange that the memorial service was scheduled so soon after his death. Logan took that opportunity to add what Tanner overheard from Mrs. Hawkins and her son – that Mr. Hawkins had not wanted to be cremated at all and her son had wanted an autopsy performed. The detective concurred that it was odd she went against her husband's wishes, but not extraordinarily so. He replied that sometimes people just want to move on with their lives as quickly as possible or just can't deal with the pain. Perhaps Mrs. Hawkins just couldn't cope with drawing out the funeral process.

Melissa agreed that burying one's spouse is difficult, but she couldn't comprehend going against a spouse's final wishes. The mere thought was mortifying to her. Jason sensed the subject was bringing up memories of when she had to bury her own husband a few years ago after his aircraft accident. Even though they had been together a while now, he knew and understood that Melissa missed Kevin with all her heart each and every day. He accepted that fact about their relationship. At this point he considered it best to change the subject, but Logan was not done.

"Jason," the young man asked, "is it true that the coroner performed an autopsy on a dead seagull from Oregon Inlet? And that there were a lot of dead seagulls there?" By the look on the older gentleman's face, Logan had his answer. Melissa looked over at his beau with confusion.

Since the death of Mr. Hawkins had been ruled due to natural causes, he determined he could tell them a little about the case that wasn't a real case. The detective explained that his partner had bagged the dead birds as evidence on a hunch. He hadn't agreed with the move, but it was done. Without asking for permission, the younger cop ordered an autopsy on the birds, since he couldn't get one of Mr. Hawkins. "It's ridiculous, really," he commented. He further reported that the chief had not been happy with Cory at all, and had ordered him to cease and desist.

Melissa was still trying to wrap her head around what dead seagulls had to do with the death of Mr. Hawkins. "Poisoned birds?" she asked almost in a whisper. "What poisoned them?" Jason didn't know and hadn't even thought to ask since he thought the whole situation was silly. Birds eat stuff they're not supposed to all the time. They could've been poisoned by just about anything. Melissa interjected, "But Cory thinks perhaps the birds ate something that Mr. Hawkins ate. He believes Mr. Hawkins was poisoned, right?"

"Yeah, I guess so," he answered. Jason was well aware what the expressions on Melissa and Logan's faces meant. They saw this as a mystery now. He knew enough to be more than a little concerned. The last thing either one of them needed was to get in the middle of an investigation. "Besides," he thought, "there is no investigation."

Melissa added, "Did anyone else think it was strange that Mr. Hawkins retired rather abruptly?" Jason rolled his eyes. It was too late. Her brain had kicked into mystery-solving mode. She continued, "Cheryl and Ronnie mentioned it today. Apparently, everyone at work was surprised and Sophie was *very* unhappy about it." Biting her lower lip as she went deep into thought, "Maybe Mr. Hawkins was too much of a liability for Johnson. He did know all the old man's dirty little secrets." After last summer's ordeal where Johnson's son tried to frame her for a murder she didn't commit, Melissa highly distrusted the elder Mr. Johnson. It wouldn't surprise her if he had illicit business dealings that perhaps Mr. Hawkins knew about. In her mind, Johnson wouldn't be above eliminating anything, or anyone, that could undermine his business or family. He had even sent that pesky lawyer to harass her and Logan after his son, Eddie, had been arrested.

That brought up another thought – that same pesky lawyer had been at the memorial service today. She remembered noting that he spoke with Mrs. Hawkins for an extended period of time. Melissa mentioned it to Jason and Logan. Something must have sparked a memory because Jason's eyes grew large at the news. He was reluctant to do so, but knew Melissa wouldn't let it go. She saw that look on his face. He knew something that he wasn't telling. "Actually," he began, "Mr. Andrews was at the precinct the other day just before the chief called Cory and me into his office for a lashing about the unapproved bird autopsy." He tried to explain that there could be any number of reasons that the attorney was meeting with the chief, but even those reasons sounded paltry to him. Jason had to admit, maybe his partner had been right. Maybe there was something more to Mr. Hawkins death than an old man having a heart attack while fishing alone. Regardless of what he thought was best, Melissa and Logan were now on the case.

Chapter 7

Life in Kill Devil Hills appeared to return to normal that week. Jason and Cory went back to working petty crime cases as the amount of pickpocketing had increased along the boardwalk since the arrival of tourists for the summer. Melissa's bakery business was bustling, so she had less time to focus on the mystery of Mr. Hawkins and the dead seagulls. Logan spent a great deal of time at the beach with Emily. He wanted so badly to help alleviate her sadness about her grandfather's death. The poor girl was taking it hard. The rest of the Hawkins family had returned back to Fairfax, VA. Yes, life in the small seaside town was back to its usual summertime routine.

Jason's partner still stewed over the chief closing the case on Mr. Hawkins so quickly. Personally, Jason wanted to forget the whole thing. The young detective just could not let it go and it was making life at the precinct more difficult. Since the case was ruled death by natural causes, all the 'evidence' should have been thrown out or returned to the Hawkins family. Being stubborn, Cory had been lax in this particular duty. The dead birds still sat in the morgue freezer, along with the food and beverages

Mr. Hawkins had taken with him to the beach that fateful day.

Early the following week, Mrs. Hawkins stopped by the police station unexpectedly. She sashayed in dressed to the nines in a designer sundress, sandals, and Coach handbag. For someone in mourning, she appeared bright and downright cheerful. Humming softly, she headed straight for the Chief of Police's office where she was immediately invited in. Jason considered this a slightly unusual since the chief always made people wait, regardless of who it was. One time he left the mayor waiting for thirty minutes as he talked on the phone with his cable provider.

Within a few minutes, the chief hollered for Jason and Cory. Both detectives shot each other a questioning look before heading over. Mrs. Hawkins smiled sweetly at them both and thanked them profusely for all their hard work on her husband's case. "The department has been so helpful and kind during this sad time that I wanted to come here in person to show my family's appreciation," she said. The two detectives thanked her for the nice comments, but Jason thought she certainly didn't give off the impression of being 'sad'. He always considered himself a good reader of persons. He could tell that was not sadness behind her smile. She was genuinely in a good mood.

The chief informed the two detectives that Mrs. Hawkins had come by to retrieve her husband's personal belongings that had been taken by the department from Oregon Inlet. Thankfully, for Cory's sake, he didn't know about the continued presence of items tucked away in the morgue. He also didn't know that the young officer had taken fingerprints off most of the items brought in from the scene. Those were hidden away in his desk for a later time. Cory planned to access the fingerprint database when he was least likely to get caught. The chief would have his head if he found out.

Jason volunteered to fetch the items for her, but Cory insisted on accompanying him. As they headed out of the office and down to the storage room. "Ok, Cory, what's up?" Jason asked. He sensed his partner's unease.

"Man, didn't it seem odd to you that the widow is all smiles and sunshine?" Cory inquired. Actually, Jason had caught that vibe and agreed with his partner. "I've never seen a woman so recently widowed appear as if she's ready for a day of partying at the yacht club. It's just weird." No doubt, Mrs. Hawkins did not give off the impression of the grieving widow. Jason tried to reason that perhaps this was just how she dealt with the pain. Not everyone experienced grief in the same way. Cory wasn't buying it. Honestly, even Jason didn't believe it.

Discussing the strange behavior of Mrs. Hawkins, the two detectives returned shortly with a couple boxes of items for the widow. Included in the boxes were Mr. Hawkins' fishing rod and reel, tackle box, cooler, beach chair, cell phone, clothes, and keys to the truck that was still in the department's impound lot. She perused through the boxes, then looked up with a perplexed look. "Detectives, where are the other items my husband took that day? There appears to be some things missing."

Confused, neither man understood what could be missing and said so. "Well, here's the cooler but where are the food and beverages that were in the cooler? I helped him pack it myself. It was loaded with all sorts of scrumptious items to keep him from growing hungry or thirsty."

Now they were really confused. Did the widow truly want the food and drinks that were in her husband's cooler? It had been well over a week. The food would've turned rotten by now anyway. There had only been a couple of empty water bottles and a half-empty can of Coors. Jason guessed everything had been tossed already. Cory even stated as much. What his partner didn't know was that he had stored the food and drinks away, along with the birds, in the morgue freezer. For whatever reason, he felt he should hang on to those things for now. He would never have suspected the widow would want them back. The chief reassured Mrs. Hawkins that the food and drinks would have been tossed out by now. He apologized that the department no longer had the items and even offered to reimburse her for the cost. After a moment's hesitation, Mrs. Hawkins smiled back at the chief with what seemed to be a look of relief to Jason. "Oh, never mind," she said, "It wasn't that important anyway." Back to her cheerful self, she asked Detective Bronson to help her carry the items to her car. In a cloud of expensive-smelling perfume, she strolled out of the precinct humming a Beatles tune.

Cory came back to his desk more perplexed than usual. "Jason, did anything about that encounter seem 'off' to you?" he asked his partner. Actually, a lot had seemed 'off', but he worried the younger cop would take that as a reason to pursue his unauthorized investigation of Mr. Hawkins' demise, so he kept his mouth shut. Cory continued though. "Did you know Mrs. Hawkins now drives a brand new Mercedes Benz convertible? I guess the old man had quite a life insurance policy." Jason shrugged, but thought it peculiar that an insurance policy would've paid out so quickly.

Later that day, Jason prepared to leave for a long lunch with Melissa when he was called back into the chief's office, along with Cory. On speakerphone was an irate Joey Hawkins, the son of the deceased. Apparently, he had a long time to think over the events since his father's death on his return trip to Virginia. He stated his disappointment that the department had so quickly closed the case and ruled it a natural death. He was especially incensed that there had not been an autopsy performed on his father's body, even if his mother had requested that one not be done. "What kind of hillbilly organization are you running where you allow the grieved widow to make that kind of call?" he asked angrily. The chief did his best to explain, but Joey was not in the mood to listen to excuses. Being a high-up bureaucrat at the State Department in Washington, D.C. gave him a sense of superiority and he was not above using his position to order others around, even little old hillbilly police departments.

Whereas, the chief and Jason were both visibly annoyed at the attitude being directed their way, Cory saw an opening. His eyes fairly gleamed as he listened to Joey's tirade. Perhaps he would get the investigation he wanted after all. The chief attempted to diffuse the situation, but failed miserably. "Mr. Hawkins, at the time there was no indication of foul play. The department considered it best for everyone to not overturn your mother's request, so an autopsy was never ordered. Even if we reopened the case, an autopsy could not be performed since your father was cremated."

This was another sore point with Joey Hawkins. "I don't care what my mother requested, officers! Did you numskulls even verify that my father wished to be cremated?" he asked. Without waiting for a response, he answered his own question, "No, of course you didn't." He continued, "Because if you had you would have read in his will that his final request was to be buried in the family plot beside his parents. I have the will right in front of me and it states that, in very clear, unambiguous language." All three police officers were dumbfounded. The chief tried to explain that the department was not responsible for what happened to the bodies of the deceased once the family claimed the body from the morgue. Jason offered that perhaps he should consult with his mother who ordered the cremation. Unfortunately, the grieved son needed someone to blame for this travesty and had chosen the police department as the scapegoat.

Detective Bronson saw his chance. Even though he knew the backlash he would get from his partner and the chief, he trudged along anyway. "Mr. Hawkins," he began, "we may not have your father's body anymore in order to perform an autopsy, but…," Jason tried to interrupt because he knew where this was going. It was too late though. "We do have the bodies of several dead seagulls that were found in the same area as your father's body." Both Jason and the chief groaned. Cory continued quickly before the other two officers could stop him, "And I'm sure, with your influence, we could get the FBI to analyze your father's ashes, if needed."

Joey Hawkins jumped on those statements. "So there was reason to believe my father's death was not from natural causes? Why did your department close the case then? Obviously, there was something amiss if you bagged dead seagulls from the scene." He ranted for a long time. The chief placed the speakerphone on mute and let into the young detective. Jason cringed as he knew he would be blamed for not curtailing his partner's enthusiasm for an investigation that the department did not deem worthy of pursuing.

The chief cut his verbal throttling of the younger man off as he heard Joey ask them a question in harsh tones. Apparently, they had missed the question earlier as he raised his voice on the other end to get their attention. By the end of the phone call, they all felt like they had been through the proverbial ringer. The chief had no choice but to agree with Joey to *quietly* reopen the case. The only one smiling in the room was Cory, who felt vindicated in his 'hunch'.

Chapter 8

An exhausted Jason showed up at Melissa's house that evening. From the moment she opened the door, she knew something was wrong. However, she was not the type to push. She simply waited. He would tell her when he was ready. That night they enjoyed a quick and light dinner as the boys planned to go fishing until dark. It was sacred bonding time between Jason and Logan. Melissa appreciated the attention Jason gave to her nephew. She knew he needed a good male role model at this precarious stage in his life. Unfortunately, she felt her brother was not fulfilling that need in Logan's life.

Shortly after the boys left, Melissa went to join her friends Cheryl and Maria for a glass or two of wine at a quaint bistro a block away from the beach. Ladies' night had not been interfered with, despite the presence of a man in her life. The women enjoyed teasing their friend about her boyfriend, but they were truly glad she had found some happiness once again. After ordering their drinks, they seated themselves at a small, round table on the second-story porch with a lovely view of the ocean.

They discussed a number of topics. Maria's eldest son had failed his economics class at NC State last semester. His summer would now be spent on campus. Cheryl had a nasty argument with the local vegetable supplier she used for her restaurant. The spinach delivered over the last several weeks had been rotten. She was in the process of finding another supplier. Melissa updated the women on Logan's visit. He spent a lot of time with Emily Hawkins. She smiled at the thought of the two teenagers. Logan had confided to her that he really, really liked the young lady. He was still too nervous to do anything more than hold her hand though. Melissa thought that was lovely. At their age, holding hands was quite enough.

At the mention of the Hawkins' granddaughter, Cheryl perked up. The expression on her face made the other two women realize there was something she wanted to add, but she held back for a while. It wasn't until she finished her second glass of the house red wine that Cheryl loosened up. "Speaking of the Hawkins family, have either of you seen Sophie lately?" Neither woman had seen the widow, but considering she just lost her husband they had not felt it was unusual. "Well," Cheryl continued, "I saw her yesterday afternoon. She was getting out of a new Mercedes convertible in front of the jewelry store on Main Street. Seems like she is wasting no time spending her poor husband's life insurance money." The women were surprised, but not too much. They realized Sophie had a taste for the finer things that had only been curtailed by her husband's income that couldn't keep up with her expensive demands. Half the town gossiped that it was his attempts to keep his wife in a lifestyle he couldn't afford that had attributed to his early demise.

The women didn't dwell on the subject of Mrs. Hawkins too long though. Maria's phone rang, interrupting their sojourn. Her husband, Luis, had a problem with their washing machine and needed her help. Apologizing to the other women, Maria reluctantly left to tend to the defunct washer. "Who says men know how to fix things? Someone needs to start a business to fix things that husbands 'fix'," she stated with a laugh. Melissa made to leave as well, but Cheryl stopped her for a moment.

"Melissa, has Jason mentioned anything about the Hawkins case to you?" she asked. Technically, cops could not discuss cases with anyone not within the department. However, since it was ruled there wasn't a case, that the man had died most likely from natural causes, they had discussed it a little. The other woman had a gleam in her eye, so Melissa suspected she knew more than she had previously let on. When questioned about it, Cheryl opened up. It didn't take much persuading. The woman loved to gossip. Her husband worked at Johnson Shipping International and had dealt with Mr. Hawkins a lot over the years. He confessed everyone was shocked when the older gentleman retired so suddenly. One day, after a heated argument with Mr. Johnson and his lead attorney, he had stormed out with a look of defeat on his face. Mr. Hawkins was as stubborn as a mule, and didn't ever concede. Ronnie couldn't imagine what would cause the old man to react so defeatist. Within the hour, an email had been sent to the entire organization announcing his retirement, effective immediately. The old man didn't even have time to clear out his desk before he was escorted from the building. "Doesn't sound like a voluntary retirement, does it?" she asked. Melissa concurred that it did not.

"It gets even more peculiar," she continued. Later that afternoon, Ronnie's assistant witnessed Mrs. Hawkins bursting into Mr. Johnson's office. Normally, someone would be thrown out of the building by security, but she wasn't. After about half an hour, she left with a big smile on her face.

"Okay," Melissa exclaimed, "that IS weird!" What on earth could Mrs. Hawkins have to say to Mr. Johnson? The old man wasn't known for being civil to anyone, so why he didn't have her tossed out immediately only added to the mystery. Melissa made a mental note to ask Jason about it later. Her curiosity was piqued as was Cheryl's who said she'd nagged her husband to find out more. Unfortunately though, Ronnie wanted no part of it. If there was something there, he didn't care; it wasn't worth losing his job over if he was caught snooping around. He valued his paycheck and his retirement account too much.

The boys returned from their moderately successful fishing excursion around 10 pm. Both were dirty and smelled of the ocean. The younger man excitedly told his aunt about the puffer fish he caught and how it 'puffed up' before heading off to take a long, hot shower. In the meantime, Jason relaxed with Melissa on the back porch. Smelling fishy, he wasn't allowed on the indoor furniture anyway. After a brief story of the fish that got away, that was "this big", she decided to just come out and ask him about Hawkins. That look of exhaustion came back over his features so she knew something was amiss. "He didn't die of natural causes, did he?" she asked. Jason assured her that Mr. Hawkins had 'probably' passed away from a heart attack or stroke or something completely normal. However, the case was being re-opened at the insistence of Hawkins' son and the meddling of his partner, Cory. Aside from that, he could no longer discuss it with her.

Although he was prohibited from telling her anything about an ongoing investigation, she filled him in on what Cheryl told her that evening.

Jason told her that he would mention it to his partner, but he still thought this whole thing was a dead end. It was his job though to follow leads. As he drove home later that evening, he inwardly cringed at the idea of having to question Mr. Edward Johnson and his attorney, Peter Andrews. Neither man was the pleasant sort. This would be just the sort of thing to set them off. After their encounters last summer over the Stevenson murder, he was not looking forward to tangling with them again.

Chapter 9

The next morning, Logan set out early to meet up with Emily for a promised surf lesson. He tried last summer to teach her, but the young woman had not mastered the art form yet. He thought it would be an excellent way to keep her mind off her grandfather's death. Her heart was broken. Logan just wanted to see the beautiful young woman smile again. The Surf Shack was not open yet, so he waited outside on the highly splintered picnic table. It was a glorious morning as the burnt orange sun peeked over the ocean's horizon. "Today is going to be perfect," he thought.

Emily tried sneaking up behind him to startle him. Although waif-like in appearance, she still had the clumsiness of an awkward teenage girl. By attempting to tiptoe over to the table, she failed to avoid a sharp seashell sticking up in the sand. Instead of silently tapping him on the shoulder, she yelped and hopped over to the table. She nearly fell on top of Logan in the process. This would have been fine with the young man. Rather than catching the damsel in distress, she plopped down beside him holding her bleeding foot. Logan examined the wound tenderly. Neither had a first-aid kit, but the boy knew the manager of The Surf Shack kept one in the back room. Unfortunately, the shop was closed at the moment. Logan decided it was worth the risk of getting in trouble, so he shimmied the back door lock. Tanner had taught him the trick last summer. He doubted the owner knew his shop was so easily broken into.

He fetched the first-aid kit and tended to Emily's bleeding foot. Logan made a great nurse. Soon the cut was cleaned and the foot wrapped in gauze. He just returned the kit to its place and closed the back door when the manager walked up. Logan casually remarked, "Good morning, Mr. Sullivan." The man grunted something similar to a "Good morning" as he opened the front door of his business to prepare for a long day of summer tourists who knew zilch about surfing. Emily and Logan barely contained their laughter as they realized they had been so close to being caught breaking and entering.

Since surf lessons were now off the agenda due to the young woman's injury, Logan offered to drive Emily over to his aunt's bakery for some fresh muffins for breakfast. She happily agreed, but needed to call her grandmother first to let her know where she was going. After the call, Logan helped his friend hop over to his scooter. He enjoyed the feel of her slight frame as she leaned against him.

The ride over to the Kill Devil Delicacies was also enjoyable as Emily wrapped her slender arms around his waist. The smile on the young man's face was priceless.

Melissa and her assistant, Maddie, had just opened the front doors of the bakery when the couple arrived. The aroma from the back room was tantalizing. Maddie had prepared her scrumptious blueberry-cheesecake muffins early that morning. The muffins were still hot when she served them to the teens with tall glasses of orange juice and bowls of cantaloupe. Melissa was in the back finishing up her loaves of lemon sage bread and cranberry orange bread. She peeked her head out of the back room. "Logan, sweetie," she began, "when you're done can you take these boxes of breadsticks and bread bowls over to Cheryl?" The poor boy cringed at the endearment, "sweetie". Emily smiled and chuckled.

Logan nearly dropped the boxes as he collided with Jason coming in the door for his morning coffee and muffin. Laughing, he helped the young man carry his load across the street. The two returned quickly. Melissa wiped her flour coated hands on her apron as she came out of the back room. There was flour in her hair so Jason teased her about going grey. She smacked him with a kitchen towel in reply. Usually, he would hang out for a while before heading into the office, but today was different. He dreaded what awaited him at the precinct, but knew Cory would already be hard at work to prove Mr. Hawkins had died of unnatural causes. In Jason's opinion, the young detective was way too enthusiastic in his determination for this to be a murder case. The older cop often thought Cory was more suited to a career in a district with far more interesting crime than what occurred in the small town of Kill Devil Hills. Reluctantly, he kissed Melissa softly on the cheek and walked briskly down the street towards the precinct.

While the others enjoyed a relaxing morning of warm muffins and conversation, Jason's experience was much more stressful. Cory greeted him with a huge Cheshire cat smile as he entered the office. "Okay, apparently you have some news," Jason stated as he plopped down in his desk chair. "Don't leave me in suspense," he ordered. Delighted to fill his partner in, Cory informed him that forensics had finished their tests on every dead seagull that had been brought in. All of them had died of a particular manufactured poison. It was such a distinctive chemical that it was mostly prohibited for use in the United States.

"Okay," Jason began, "how do we connect the poisoned birds to the dead body of Mr. Hawkins?"

He continued, "Do we know how the birds came to ingest the poison?" The younger detective gleamed as he related the rest of his story. Forensics found the poison had been contained in snippets of bread that the birds ate. Other pickings of trash from the ocean or seashore that the birds ate did not contain the poison.

At this point, Cory's expression became more reserved. He knew something more, but somehow was reluctant to just come out with it. After a few moments of contemplative silence, the younger man confided in a hushed tone, "There was bread found with Mr. Hawkins' things. It was lemon sage bread from the Kill Devil Delicacies bakery. Forensics is testing the bread now to determine if it's the same bread that killed the birds." Jason's heart nearly stopped. Kill Devil Delicacies was his girlfriend's bakery. Lemon sage bread was one her most famous specialties. At this point, it appeared Melissa could be a suspect in another murder if it was proven that Mr. Hawkins consumed the bread. All he could think was that they had just gone through a similar set of circumstances last summer. He knew she couldn't possibly have poisoned anyone, but that didn't mean she couldn't be considered a suspect. Jason also knew that he would most likely be removed from the case if the bread was found to be poisoned. Off the case, his hands would be tied and he would be unable to help exonerate her…again.

Chapter 10

It had been one of the worst days of his long career with the Kill Devil Hills police department. Ever since Cory dropped the bombshell this morning about the poisoned bread found in the gullets of the dead seagulls, he had felt ill. Most of the day he spent waiting. Mostly he waited on forensics to complete their tests. Cory apparently kept a lot of Mr. Hawkins' things from Oregon Inlet. None of which the young detective had told his partner or his boss about. The chief was furious with him, and with Jason for not knowing about it.

The chief had only agreed to open the case quietly so as not to alert the news press or incur the wrath of Mrs. Hawkins. However, that idea was blown to bits when the Channel 9 news crew showed up with blaring lights and a loud reporter demanding answers. He trusted that no one in the department had notified the media. No, this was Joey Hawkins' way of manipulating the department to step up their game. The chief cursed the man as he instructed his assistant to schedule a department press conference for later that afternoon.

That wasn't the only reason to fling curses at Mr. Hawkins' son. By midday, a nerdy looking man in his thirties arrived bearing a pocket protector, large briefcase, and a FBI badge. Joey had sent him there to conduct his own evaluations of the evidence. "Just the headache I need," the chief fumed, "a Fed getting in the way." He barked at Cory to find the agent suitable office space to conduct his investigation. What had been ruled death by natural causes was now a media circus complete with a know-it-all Federal agent. Early retirement was looking good to the chief about then.

The press conference went about as well as could be expected. The chief informed the public that some evidence had come to light that 'may' indicate Mr. Williams Hawkins did not die of natural causes as had been previously ruled. He announced that the lead detective on the case was Cory Bronson and that he would be working closely with Mr. Elijah Young, a FBI agent on assignment from Washington, DC. The information that the FBI was now involved triggered a storm of questions that the chief gladly passed along to Cory. The astute young reporter from Channel 9 piped up to ask why the senior detective, Jason Payne, was not the lead on the case. Both the chief and Jason cringed. The chief did not want it known to the public that the detective was dating a probable suspect so he claimed "No comment." Actually, the rest of the press conference questions were answered either as "No comment" or "We cannot comment at this time due to this is an ongoing investigation". Cory seemed to enjoy the three ring circus which he'd started. Jason knew this was the young cop's chance to shine. He just wished he didn't have to do it at his lady love's expense.

It didn't take long for the news to spread about the investigation. The news stations had covered the press conference live. Within half an hour, the phones were all lit up. Finally, the chief instructed his assistant to either direct calls to Detective Bronson or to just let it go to voicemail. There was one call he had to take though – the call from Mrs. Sophie Hawkins. The widow was highly displeased with the course of events. Her ear-splitting rampage was heard throughout the office as the chief had to place the receiver down on his desk. Her shrieking was so painful he could not hold the phone to his ear. As she ranted, the chief rubbed his throbbing temples and choked back two more Excedrin for his headache.

Jason thought the chief's day couldn't possibly get any worse. He was wrong. The Johnson's attorney, Peter Andrews, stopped by for a visit. Although he considered it peculiar for the man to be interested in the investigation, he shrugged it off. Nothing about this case made any sense anyway. Jason couldn't hear what was being said in the enclosed office, but he could see the exasperated look on his boss's face. Cory even remarked how extraordinary it was to have such an eclectic group of people interested in Mr. Hawkins' death. The younger detective certainly seemed to be enjoying himself with all the fuss swirling around the department now. Jason thought sarcastically to himself, "Will serve him right when it comes out Mr. Hawkins did die of natural causes."

Just as Jason was about to leave for the day, his partner rushed over to his desk. Cory had spent the majority of the afternoon with the FBI guy, Elijah Young. They had taken over the forensics lab and ran tests of all the items still in police custody. At some point, someone would have to reclaim the items that were already given back to Mrs. Hawkins. Jason vowed that someone would not be him. Without so much as a word, Cory yanked Jason away to the lab. Once the door closed behind them, he excitedly explained that they had discovered how the birds, and probably Mr. Hawkins, were poisoned. Grinning from ear to ear, he held up a brown paper bag with the label, "Kill Devil Delicacies", emblazoned on the front. Considering Jason's girlfriend owned and operated the bakery, Cory should have been a tad more couth about his announcement. At this point, the young detective was beyond caring. He finally had the proof to show everyone that he was right all along. The bread was poisoned. The seagulls died from the poison. Therefore, Mr. Hawkins likely died of the poison as well. He was right! That was all that mattered to him.

Jason asked the FBI agent to corroborate Cory's pronouncement. He simply nodded 'yes'. Agent Young then suggested they allow him to finish his report so they could all go into the chief's office together with their findings. Jason inquired if there were any other findings. Cory and the agent both nodded excitedly. Fingerprints were obtained from Mr. Hawkins' cell phone. The elder detective was curious how they were able to analyze fingerprints on the phone since they had given it back to Mrs. Hawkins already. Cory at least had the good sense to hang his head a little in shame as he admitted he had taken the fingerprints off the phone and a beach chair before Mrs. Hawkins had taken the deceased man's belongings. Jason groaned at the audacity of his partner, but honestly he wasn't surprised anymore. "So whose fingerprints were on the items?" he asked. Agent Young replied that both the phone and the chair had prints that belonged to Logan Jones, the nephew of the woman who owned the bakery that had provided the poisoned bread.

Chapter 11

After arguing with his boss for over an hour, Jason admitted defeat. Although the chief thought it was preposterous that Melissa and/or Logan had anything to do with Mr. Hawkins death, he had a duty to the Hawkins family to pull them both in for questioning, at the very least. Jason would remain on the case for the time being, but would not be allowed to be present during their respective interviews. Detective Bronson was already on his way to pick them both up. Jason could only imagine the horror they would feel being interrogated about yet another possible murder. He personally took it upon himself to call Logan's parents to let them know what was happening. John David Jones was not pleased his son was in trouble with the Kill Devil Hills police department again. Jason assured him that it was simply for questioning since Logan had found the body of the dead man. He promised to have Logan call him when he finished up with the detective. The father gruffly said "Thanks" and hung up the phone.

Melissa and Logan were indeed shocked to be brought in for questioning…again. It was déjà vu of last summer completely. Logan was taken to a separate interview room where a representative from Social Services waited to be with him during questioning. Melissa was angry. She should be the one sitting at the table with Logan. She was technically his guardian while he was in town. Her brother had even seen fit to send her legal documents giving her authority over Logan's well-being during his visits. She could legally seek medical help for him, authorize an operation, or anything else a parent could do for their child. Not being allowed to support her nephew seemed ridiculous.

"Excuse me, Detective Bronson," Melissa began, "I believe I should be in the interview with my minor nephew." At the scowl on his face, she continued, "If that is not possible, then I insist that he not be asked anything until my attorney can be here with him." She'd learned from last summer. When they had initially been questioned about the death of Mrs. Stevenson, they had been entitled to have an attorney present. This time, she intended to make sure of it.

"Mrs. Maples, we just have some routine questions about Mr. Hawkins' death. Logan found the body, so we need to speak with him. It's simply a routine procedure," Cory tried to assure her. She wasn't to be fooled though. They had interviewed Logan immediately after he found Mr. Hawkins' body. As she recalled, he had been held up a long time answering their questions that day. They already had his statement. This was something more. Melissa was fiercely protective of her nephew. This time she insisted on either being in the room when he was questioned or having their lawyer in there with him. Detective Bronson relented. They did legally have a right for the presence of a lawyer. He ushered her over to his desk so she could make a call.

Melissa noticed Jason was nowhere to be found. "Shouldn't he be here?" she wondered. The other end of the phone line rang twice before a husky female voice answered, "Janice Littleton, Attorney at Law, how many I help you?" Melissa filled her attorney in quickly and hung up the phone. With a smile, she informed the detective that her lawyer was on her way. The young woman's office was just a few blocks away. In just a few minutes, Janice Littleton stormed into the precinct looking for her client. After the fiasco last summer, she was on guard for any shenanigans from the cops to railroad her client. She particularly despised Jason's former partner, Larry Reynolds, for the way he treated Melissa and Logan. She wouldn't allow Jason's new 'punk' partner to follow in that grumpy geezer's footsteps.

Janice greeted her client with a big, warm hug. She muttered under her breath, "What the devil is going on this time?" Melissa shook her head sadly and rolled her eyes. While she had waited for her attorney, the chief had come out of his office to explain that Jason had been sent home because he could not have anything to do with the interview since he was close to Melissa and Logan. However, he did hand her a note from Jason. It indicated that he was sorry he couldn't be there to support her, but knew she would understand the reason. He also wrote that he contacted Logan's father already. "Your brother was not thrilled to hear from me, of course. But I assured him that I would take care of you and Logan," the note read. Trying not to appear disappointed, Melissa shrugged and tucked the note into her jeans pocket.

With the arrival of her attorney, Melissa was escorted to an empty interview room. They were allowed a few moments to converse before Janice ordered her to not say a thing while she went into the adjacent room to be there with Logan. "Not a problem," Melissa stated.

Logan had been left in the tiny room with the Social Services representative. He appeared fine physically, but shaken and confused otherwise. He didn't understand why the cops needed to talk to him again. A few moments later, Detective Bronson entered the room with a glance over at the two-way mirror. Janice really wanted to roll her eyes at the brazen young cop. He clearly made a mistake calling in Logan and Melissa to question them about the death of Mr. Hawkins, who everyone knew died of a heart attack or something. Cory took a seat across the small table from the teenage boy and his attorney. He had a manila folder in his hand which he opened, along with a clear plastic bag containing a cell phone.

Cory began, "Logan, do you know why we brought you in today?" Logan shook his head that he didn't. The detective continued by asking if the boy heard that the death of Mr. Hawkins was now being investigated as a suspicious death. Logan shrugged his shoulders. He had heard, but he didn't understand what it had to do with him. The young man even asked the detective point blank why they needed to talk to him again. They had his statement from earlier. Nothing changed since he spoke with them that day. His attorney interjected that the detective better have a good reason for needing to question her client again. Otherwise, the boy should be allowed to go home.

The detective looked behind him at the two-way mirror again. "Detective," Janice stated, "please make your point or stop wasting my client's time. If you need to consult with your cohort behind the glass, then please do so." In response, Cory laid the plastic bag with the cell phone on the table and asked Logan if he recognized it. The boy nodded and answered that it was Mr. Hawkins' cell phone. The detective then pulled out a piece of paper from his folder. He informed Logan that it was a report from the forensics department. "Can you get to the point, officer?" Janice requested irritably.

"We found two sets of fingerprints on the phone. One set belonged to Mr. Hawkins, of course," the detective replied. "The other set of prints belonged to Mr. Logan Jones. Now, son, how did your fingerprints get on Mr. Hawkins' phone?" Well, that was quite simple actually. The teenager repeated his story from the first time he told it when he found Mr. Hawkins at Oregon Inlet. Logan grabbed the phone to call 911. He stated that he found it next to the dead man's body.

"Alright then, I believe that may be in your earlier statement," the detective concurred. "However, can you explain how your fingerprints came to be all over the beach chair?" he asked as he showed the boy a picture of it. Logan explained that when he first arrived at the beach, he saw the beach chair was being washed out to sea by the waves. He saved the chair and then went to find its owner. That was when he discovered Mr. Hawkins lying in the sand.

Detective Bronson then showed Logan and Janice pictures of a dead seagull. "Did you happen to notice there were several dead birds scattered along Oregon Inlet that day?" he asked. Janice was bewildered by the strange question. The boy stated that he hadn't noticed. He was, after all, rather spooked after finding Mr. Hawkins not breathing and without a pulse so maybe they were there. He just didn't pay any attention to it at the time.

Janice had reached the end of her patience with the detective. He was asking questions to which he already knew the answers. Now he was showing disgusting pictures of dead seagulls. "What, may I ask, do these dead birds have to do with my client?" she asked. That was when Cory dropped the big news. There were several dead seagulls along Oregon Inlet that day. He proudly announced that he had bagged the birds on a hunch. Janice and Logan resisted the urge to roll their eyes at that nugget of news. The detective's blue eyes flashed as he revealed the kicker – the birds had all died of poison. The attorney and the teenager both looked at him blankly. Finally, Janice broke the silence. "So what?"

Cory stood up and excused himself for a moment. He came back in shortly thereafter with another clear plastic bag. He placed the bag on the table. "Logan, do you recognize this?" he asked smugly. The boy's eyes grew big. Janice also noticed the bag's contents and understood. Logan nodded. "Can you tell me what that is, son?" the detective continued. Logan nodded again. He saw similar items just about every day. It was a brown paper bag from her aunt's bakery. It even had "Kill Devil Delicacies" written on the top in overly dramatic cursive. Cory continued, "Forensic tests confirmed that the same poison that killed the birds was also in the loaf of bread in this particular bag." The young man and the attorney could connect the dots. The cops, at least this cop, believed that Mr. Hawkins also ate the bread and that was what killed him. Apparently, it was too much of a coincidence that bread from his aunt's bakery was poisoned and he happened to find the body. Detective Bronson didn't seem to believe any further explanation was needed as he ended the interview at that point.

Janice exited the interview room after instructing Logan to keep his mouth shut. The boy was highly agitated that the cops would dare think he or his aunt had anything to do with the death of Mr. Hawkins. Considering how much Aunt Mel loved all animals, especially birds, it was preposterous to think she would do anything to endanger or kill the birds. She loved birds! Birds fly and her late husband loved to fly. He didn't want her upset if the stupid cop showed her pictures of the poor feathered creatures. The attorney assured him everything would be fine as she went to discuss the situation with Melissa before she was questioned.

Melissa was evidently concerned about what had taken so long with Logan. She wanted confirmation that he was okay before she would listen to anything Janice had to say. Once the attorney filled her in on what transpired during Logan's interview, Melissa was shocked; silent. Detective Bronson didn't give her much time though. He burst into the room ready to grill her as well. The interview went much the same as the earlier one, minus the questions about the cell phone and beach chair. She answered as best as she could:

- Yes, she recognized the paper bag. It was from her bakery.
- Yes, her bakery did sell the type of bread listed on the label – lemon sage bread. It was one of her specialties.
- No, she had no idea how bread from her shop would have been poisoned.

- No, she had no knowledge of poisons other than what to spray around the house to keep the extra-large spiders from getting inside.
- No, she didn't sell the bread directly to Mr. Hawkins. His wife always bought bread from her, usually once a week.
- No, she didn't recall if Mrs. Hawkins had purchased bread that week. She could check the receipts though.
- Yes, she knew Logan planned to fish the morning in question at Oregon Inlet.
- No, she had no idea Mr. Hawkins retired earlier that week.
- No, she did not know Mr. Hawkins would be fishing at Oregon Inlet that day.

Cory questioned her for over an hour. She answered precisely the same every time he repeated a question. Melissa was just as puzzled how a loaf of bread from her shop came to be poisoned. That just didn't make any sense. After she promised to turn over her business receipts for the last six weeks, the detective informed her that she was free to go. He added that she shouldn't leave town in the near future though. Janice escorted Melissa from the interview room and grabbed Logan on the way out. Frustrated and bewildered, the trio headed over to Janice's office to discuss the strange case. The attorney was more than a little concerned about her client and friend. Melissa and Logan were just as perplexed. Sadly, they knew their only source of information that could help them figure things out was Jason. Being a cop though, Melissa knew he would be unable to discuss the case. She and Logan were on their own.

Chapter 12

Melissa checked her phone on the walk over to the attorney's office. Jason left a voice mail message apologizing for not being there with her and Logan at the precinct. His boss had him under 'lock and key' since he was known to be in a relationship with her. She sighed with annoyance. Logan asked what was wrong, but Melissa just shook her head.

After settling into a small conference room in the attorney's office space, both Melissa and Logan explained every fact that they knew about the death of Mr. William Hawkins. Janice had already heard most of it, but wanted their sides of the story. They all agreed it was peculiar. The attorney assured her clients that, so far, the police did not have a lot to go on. That was in their favor. At this point, they couldn't even prove Mr. Hawkins was poisoned despite the dead seagulls. The bread was Melissa's only connection to the case. The only thing connecting Logan was that he found Mr. Hawkins dead. However, finding a dead person was not a crime. Janice was confident Logan was completely in the clear. However, Melissa was another matter. How did her bread become poisoned? They needed to know at what point the bread was poisoned. If after baking, then she was fine. Anyone could have introduced the poison after baking though.

What really bothered the young lawyer was there was no motive whatsoever for Melissa to want Mr. Hawkins dead. In that aspect, the police department had nothing. Melissa admitted she barely knew the man. He never even came to her bakery. She only ever saw his wife. Mrs. Hawkins came into the shop fairly often. Logan was friends with their granddaughter, Emily. Otherwise, they had no connection to the family whatsoever. After she jotted down some notes from their conversation, Janice encouraged them both to go about their daily lives. If the cops called on them again, they should have her number on speed dial. "One last thing…can your boyfriend help us out with any additional information about the case? I doubt Detective Sunshine told us everything they know today," Janice asked. Sadly, Melissa didn't believe Jason would be allowed to help them. The attorney drove them home. Just in case reporters had been informed the two had been hauled into the police department for questioning, she didn't want them harassed.

Later that night, Melissa cooked 'breakfast for dinner'. Biscuits and gravy with sausage links and eggs served as comfort food for the duo. Afterwards, they decided the best way to get their minds off their current dilemma was to 'veg' in front of the television. That was a huge mistake. The local news popped up on the screen first. The same obnoxious reporter from News Channel 9 conducted an interview with Joseph Hawkins, the son of the deceased Mr. Hawkins.

The younger Hawkins spoke eloquently about his beloved father and his love for his family. His tone changed to one of anger as he verbally throttled the Kill Devil Hills police department for the rushed determination that his father died of natural causes. He admitted to the reporter that the police would never have reopened the case if he hadn't threatened them to do it. "Good thing I did that. Otherwise, we never would have discovered my father was actually poisoned with a loaf of my mother's favorite bread from the Kill Devil Delicacies – lemon sage bread. The proprietor, Melissa Maples, poisoned my father with her bread. Just last summer she was suspected of killing someone else. Somehow, she got out from under those charges. She will NOT be so lucky this time," Joey Hawkins ranted.

Logan grabbed the remote control and hit the power button. The two sat in stunned silence for a long time. Within minutes, Melissa's home phone began to ring. The shrill tone of the house phone startled them from their reverie. They were both afraid to answer the phone. Just as she was about to pick up the receiver, her cell phone blared her ring tone – "Sweet Home Alabama". Flustered, she motioned for Logan to let the home phone go to voicemail as she checked the caller id on her cell phone. It was her brother, John David. Taking a deep breath, she answered. Logan could tell the conversation was not going well, even though he just heard one side of it. The home phone began to ring again. Again, Melissa indicated to Logan to not answer it.

Eventually, she handed her cell phone to Logan so he could talk with his father. As the home phone began ringing yet again, Melissa decided to risk answering it. Of course, it was a news reporter. She replied calmly, "No comment". She hung up the phone and immediately unplugged it from the wall. Logan's father informed the boy that he was coming out to the shore to pick him up. The teenager explained to his dad that the cops would not allow him to leave the area. Besides, there was no way he was leaving Aunt Mel during this craziness. His aunt interrupted that perhaps it was best if Logan went back home to Charlotte, NC. He exerted his stubborn streak – a common trait in the Jones family. He refused to leave her. Together they would get to the bottom of this fiasco.

John David, for the first time in years, really listened to his son. He agreed Logan could stay, but they were going to have another guest. He was coming out there to check things out for himself. Besides, he argued, if Aunt Mel needed help then there was no one better to do so than her own brother. Logan wasn't so sure his mom would agree to all this, but his dad told him not to worry about her. Mom was on a business trip in Chicago for a couple weeks anyway. As he hung up the phone, Logan smiled.

All was quiet in the small cottage for a few minutes. Logan and Melissa both were overwhelmed after the call with John David. The silence was broken suddenly as someone knocked on the front door. "Oh dear," Melissa fretted, "It's probably the reporters already." She peeked out a small window in the kitchen to try getting a look at who was at her front door before she made the mistake of opening it. Relief flooded over her as she saw one of her best friends, Cheryl, and her husband. The couple rushed through the door as it opened. Cheryl hugged her friend tightly. Ronnie muttered something about the news vans causing a traffic mess on the way over.

Cheryl took charge of everything. She ordered Melissa and Logan to sit down and relax while she prepared some chamomile tea for them. Ronnie informed his wife that Melissa may need something stronger than tea. She agreed and instructed him where to find a bottle of red wine and a cork screw. Logan, however, could only have the tea. Within a few minutes, the group congregated in the living room to discuss the day's events. Melissa retold the story of being hauled into the precinct and questioned by Jason's partner. She explained what the cops had discovered about the seagulls being poisoned and that the poison apparently came from bread from her bakery. "Now, they've expounded on the poisoned birds to suggest that Mr. Hawkins was poisoned, too."

Ronnie perked up a bit at the mention of the poison. He asked, "Did the cops indicate what poison specifically?" Melissa shook her head. Cheryl's husband further explained that the rumor at work was that Hawkins had not exactly retired early, but had been forced out of the company. Some speculated it was because he knew too much about Johnson's misdeeds and had threatened to go public with it. No one knew for sure what Hawkins held over Johnson's head, but it had to be something bad. For years, Hawkins had been the one to clean up Johnson's messes and cover up illicit deals. It would have to be something pretty explosive for the old man to be pushed out the door.

"Okay, but what does that have to do with Hawkins being found dead, and possibly poisoned?" Logan asked. Ronnie further explained that after Mr. Hawkins' sudden retirement, Mrs. Hawkins had come into the office fuming. Her shrieks were heard throughout several floors of the tall office complex. Apparently, she was not too happy about her husband's retirement. However, she left with a huge smile on her face. Everyone thought Hawkins had his job back. That wasn't the case though. No mention was ever made that he would return to the company. A few days later, he's dead.

Well, that was all interesting. However, Melissa and Logan didn't see how Hawkins' early retirement played into his death. Cheryl prodded Ronnie to continue. He seemed reluctant to add more, but the story needed to be told. "Due to my lovely wife's 'encouragement', I decided to check around to see what Hawkins worked on prior to these events," he stated with some emphasis on 'encouragement'. What he discovered was indeed interesting and pertinent. Mr. Hawkins had been working to obscure the company's involvement with a small holding company out of the Caribbean. This company dealt with a weed killer that used a poison that was deemed illegal in most countries throughout the world. There was even a recent case of a father and his children who visited their vacation home in the islands, but shortly thereafter were found unconscious. Bloodwork showed a particular poison in their systems. An investigation discovered the landscapers for their residence used the weed killer manufactured by the holding company in question. Thankfully, the family recovered. However, they faced a long road to complete rehabilitation as the poison damaged their cardiovascular systems extensively.

Ronnie did not have definitive proof that Hawkins was run out of Johnson Shipping International because of his knowledge of, or objection to, the holding company. Basically, it was pure speculation at this point. However, if the poison in the bread was determined to be this same poison, then it was likely Mr. Johnson decided retirement wasn't enough to silence Hawkins.

Melissa's head reeled at the possibility that Edward Johnson, Sr. could be behind the death of Mr. Hawkins. Just last summer, his son was found guilty of manslaughter in the investigation of Linda Stevenson's death. The death that had occurred in her bakery and she had been arrested as the primary suspect. Little Eddie Johnson, Jr. was currently serving time in the state penitentiary in Raleigh for the crime. Now Daddy Johnson may be involved in another suspicious death. If so, was he seeking revenge for his son's arrest by framing her for Mr. Hawkins' murder?

Chapter 13

Melissa woke up the next morning with a splitting headache. The events of yesterday had taken their toll. She had lain awake most of the night as her mind raced through all the possibilities that may have led to Mr. Hawkins' death. Most importantly, she rehashed all the ways she had been roped into this fiasco. Unable to take the intensity of the migraine that set in, she gulped back two migraine pills with a glass of water and returned to bed.

Logan decided to clean up the house a little before his father arrived that afternoon. He admitted he was nervous about Dad becoming involved in all this chaos. However, he also admitted to himself that he was happy about it, too. He couldn't recall the last time his dad took a vacation from work, much less to spend time with him. The young boy realized that the circumstances weren't ideal, being neck deep in a murder investigation, but he would take whatever attention he could get from his dad.

After making up the guest bedroom and cleaning the kitchen, Logan stepped out onto the back deck to make a call. Frankly, he was more nervous about the call than his dad's impending arrival. He knew he had to do it though. He had to speak to Emily. Considering the media circus from yesterday, he didn't expect she would give him the time of day if she believed any of that garbage. Regardless, he had to at least try to get her to understand that neither he nor his aunt had anything to do with her grandfather's death. As he listened to the phone ring, he held his breath. Silently he prayed, "Please, just answer the phone."

A raspy voice, as if the person had been crying a lot, answered "Hello". It nearly broke Logan's heart to hear it. Without thinking, he asked how she was doing. The exasperated sigh on her end of the line let him know it was a ridiculous question. How was she supposed to be doing? Emily politely answered anyway. After an awkward silence, she asked wearily, "Logan, what do you want?"

Honestly, he wasn't sure what he wanted. He knew he wanted her to be okay. He knew he wanted to make her pain go away. He wanted a lot of things, but right now couldn't find his voice to say as much. "I just needed to know you were okay. With everything that's happened, I kind of figured you would be upset, angry, sad….," his voice trailed off as he tried to find the right words.

"Logan, I don't know how I'm feeling right now. No, I'm not okay. My grandfather is dead. Just a day or two ago, we believed he died of a heart attack while fishing. That was rather comforting to know that he passed away doing something he really loved. Now, the news reported that the cops believe he was murdered. To add to that, it was more than insinuated that you and your aunt had something to do with it! I'm confused! I'm heartbroken! I don't know what to believe or think right now," she ended with a heart-wrenching sob.

Logan wanted to cry right along with her. He reassured her that neither he nor his aunt had anything to do with her beloved grandfather's death. He pleaded with her to believe him. They had no reason to want to hurt anyone, much less kill someone. The young man swore he especially would never do anything that would hurt Emily. He truly cared about her and valued their friendship.

She acknowledged that the idea that they killed her grandfather with poisoned bread seemed ridiculous. Besides, the only evidence the cops had were dead seagulls. "How bizarre is that?" she asked. Emily didn't want to believe her grandfather was killed. Her grandmother certainly didn't put any faith in the accusation. She even remarked how the news had agitated her grandmother so badly that she had

103

ranted for hours last night. There had been a huge argument when her father arrived back at the house. Both had calmed down somewhat this morning, but things were definitely tense in the household.

The two teenagers discussed the situation at length, but could not come up with any answers. Logan was so relieved Emily believed in him, that he was on cloud nine when they hung up the phone. He went back inside just as the front door bell rang. Nervous that it could be reporters again or the cops, he peered out a side window first. It was his dad! "He must've sped the entire way if he's already here," he thought.

The look on John David Jones face as his son opened the door was one of both fatigue and tension. He stepped inside and caught his son up in a huge bear hug. Logan realized his father had not done that since he was a small boy. He tried not to weep as he tightly squeezed his dad back. The young man was always worried that his dad would be disappointed if he didn't always act like a "man". Up until last year, Logan rebelled from that notion. He gave his parents a hard time regarding everything. Last summer had changed him. His parents had noticed their son seemed more responsible, less troublesome. They just hadn't taken the time to let Logan know they had noticed.

Melissa appeared in the hallway just as the two men moved further into the house. Logan offered to take his dad's suitcase to the guestroom as the brother and sister greeted each other. After a long overdue hug, John David pulled away and looked into his beloved sister's face. "Migraine, huh? I can't imagine why," he remarked. He always could tell when Melissa's headaches had set in, even when she tried to hide the agonizing pain she was in. She assured him she would be fine. The medicine hadn't done the job as fast as she would have liked, but hopefully a tall dose of caffeine would assist.

The three family members settled down in the kitchen as the coffee brewed and Logan scrambled eggs. Melissa and Logan filled John David in on the events as they understood them. The young man added that he spoke with Emily that morning and that she and her grandmother believed they had nothing to do with Mr. Hawkins' death. His father scowled as he reprimanded his son for contacting the young girl in the first place. If she wasn't convinced of his innocence in the matter, she could easily try to illicit information from him that could be used against him later. Neither Logan nor Aunt Mel believed Emily would do that, but still they realized they should be more cautious in the future. John David glanced over at his sister. He hated to ask, but it was important. "Mel, any word from that cop beau of yours? Is he going to be a help or a hindrance in proving your innocence?" It was a valid question. Honestly, she wasn't sure. Aside from the voicemail yesterday after she had been questioned at the precinct, she hadn't heard from him at all.

Over at the Hawkins' residence, Emily camped out in her room to avoid both her father and her grandmother. Things were still tense between the mother and son. Joey was convinced his mom was ignoring the obvious that his dad was murdered just because it was inconvenient for her. With the case re-opened, the insurance company wouldn't cut the check to her for the life insurance. Sophie Hawkins was angered that her son wouldn't just accept the fact that William died of natural causes. She failed to comprehend why he insisted that it was something else. Emily just wanted to hide from them both.

Joey left mid-morning to visit the police department to see what else they had uncovered. The loud slam of the front door shook the entire house. Just as Emily was about to emerge from her room, she heard Sophie on the phone in the office next to her bedroom. According to the shrill tone in her voice, she could tell Grandma was upset and letting someone have a big piece of her mind. Curious,

Emily put her ear up to the wall. Didn't help much. She still could only make out a few muffled words. What she did overhear made her nervous. Sophie threatened whoever was on the other end of the line that they better fix this NOW, or she would… Drats! Emily couldn't make out the rest of what was said. "She would what?" she pondered.

A few moments later, there was a soft knock on her bedroom door. The young woman decided to not let on that she heard anything. She pretended the knocking had just woke her up. Rubbing her eyes, she opened the door. Grandma Sophie was all smiles as she greeted her grandchild. She informed Emily that there was plenty of scrambled eggs and bacon left over from breakfast if she were hungry. However, she needed to run some errands so she would see the young woman in a little while. After reassuring her grandmother that she would be fine alone, Sophie hurried out.

Emily couldn't get the conversation she "sort of" overheard out of her head. Everything since her grandfather's death had just been weird, to say the least. Instead of sitting around moping, she decided to take action. She didn't really believe her grandfather was murdered. She didn't believe, even if he had been murdered, that Logan or his aunt had anything to do with it. Now her dad was on the warpath and her usually sweet southern belle grandmother was issuing threats to persons unknown over the phone.

With the house to herself, she headed to the office next to her bedroom. Oddly, the room was locked. Her grandparents never locked any room in the house. Undeterred, Emily grabbed a hair pin from her vanity dresser. Along with fishing and surfing last summer, Logan taught her how to pick locks. His preferred method involved the use of credit cards, but she had to make do with what she had. Apparently, she was an apt pupil as it took no time to unlock the door.

Her grandfather's things were still everywhere. This had been his hideaway from his wife for most of their marriage. Family pictures hung on the walls, as well as pictures of enormous fish he caught over the years. The sailfish he reeled in when he vacationed in Mexico was his favorite, she knew.

Emily had no idea what to look for, so she chose to rifle through the desk first. On top of the desk was a copy of his life insurance policy. Glancing over the document, it was the usual legal jargon that made most legal documents difficult to understand for anyone other than lawyers. Being a young teenager, most of it didn't make sense to Emily. However, she understood the paragraph that had been highlighted, most likely by her grandmother. It read that in the event of suicide or if the insured died of suspicious causes, the insurance company had the right and authority to deny release of funds to the beneficiary until a judicial ruling absolving the beneficiary of any wrongdoing could be obtained. It was in such miniscule type that Emily had to squint to read it. She sat back in the oversized desk chair. "So that's why Grandma is so upset. She can't get her hands on his life insurance money yet," she thought with dismay. "If she's so concerned about getting the money, why is she spending money like there's no tomorrow." Sophie's uptick of extravagance had not gone unnoticed by her granddaughter. Emily considered that perhaps that was her grandmother's way of dealing with grief.

Disappointed that her grandmother may be more concerned about getting her hands on the life insurance money rather than finding out the truth about what happened, Emily continued to snoop around. She found nothing else of interest in the desk so she moved to the filing cabinet in the closet. Surprisingly, it was locked. Emily put her new lock picking skills to work again. Seemed to be mostly work-related files, but she perused them anyway. There was one file that seemed out of place. It was marked by a red label with the words, "J Chemical

Holding Company". She pulled the folder out and sat back down at the desk to read over it. What she discovered shocked her. Her grandfather left detailed notes in his own decrepit handwriting regarding his advice to his employer to extract himself from a certain holding company. The company produced a weed killer that contained a chemical illegal in most countries, including the United States. Attached to the notes were news articles about people getting deathly ill after coming in contact with the poison. Some survived their exposure to the chemical, while others in less developed countries did not. It was a publicity nightmare waiting to happen, according to her grandfather. His notes included his boss' rejection of the idea. William Hawkins seemed to believe Mr. Johnson was more concerned about his profits than the ramifications of being involved with a company known to deal with illegal chemicals that could seriously harm people or even kill them. His last notes indicated how he planned to give Johnson one last chance to do the right thing or he was going to the Federal authorities with the information.

Just as Emily finished reading the notes in the folder, she heard the front door slam as her father returned from his visit to the police station. The young woman made a split second decision as to what she needed to do with the information she just found. "Hey, Dad," she called out, "Can you come here for a minute?"

Chapter 14

Back at the police station, Jason was being kept in the dark about everything involving the case from now on. Cory and the chief apologized, but both considered his relationship with Mrs. Maples a liability. Besides, after the heated discussion with Joey Hawkins that morning, even Jason realized it was a bad situation all around. For the duration of the investigation, Jason was on traffic duty along Highway 158 as tourists flooded into and out of the seaside town. He picked up his phone countless times to call Melissa, but every time he chickened out. When she needed him the most, he couldn't help her.

Jason's partner and the FBI agent kept busy though. The chief had been furious when he discovered just how much physical evidence the younger detective had kept hidden. Not only were the corpse drawers in the morgue packed with dead seagulls, but Cory managed to talk the coroner into taking blood and tissue samples from Mr. Hawkins' dead body. None of these things had been authorized. The chief did not like being disobeyed. However, considering Joey Hawkins was breathing down his neck, he was marginally grateful.

The blood work came back negative for the poison, but the ambitious detective wouldn't give up. What he really needed was tissue samples from the dead man's stomach contents. That wasn't going to happen though. Swabs of the inside of Mr. Hawkins' mouth had not revealed any trace of the poison either. The last item they had to test was Mr. Hawkins' fingerprint. As Cory read the test results he nearly jumped for joy. There was a tiny trace of the poison embedded in the fingerprint.

Cory spent the remainder of the morning fast-tracking search warrants for Melissa's home and business. Jason happened to stroll into the precinct as his partner and the FBI agent rushed out. He may not be involved in the case, but he could recognize the signs of search warrants about to be served, as Cory called for three more uniformed cops to follow him. Realizing he could get in big trouble, he picked up his phone again. This time he finished dialing Melissa's cell phone number.

As she finished her short conversation with Jason on the phone, she informed her brother and nephew that the cops were about to execute search warrants of her home and bakery. "But act surprised," she warned them. Within a half hour, the knock came to her front door. Detective Bronson led the investigation of her home. Most of their focus was the kitchen. Her utensils and some of her baking ingredients were bagged and tagged as evidence. "At least this time," she thought, "the cops didn't leave her home in complete shambles." John David was livid, but Melissa ordered him to keep his mouth shut. It was best if they just allowed the police to do whatever they needed to do so they would leave sooner rather than later. Detective Bronson informed her a search was also being conducted at the Kill Devil Delicacies bakery. He even offered that she could tag along to observe their search in case she was worried about them trashing her business. Melissa surprised herself by taking him up on the offer. However, she refused to ride in a police squad car. Instead, her brother dropped her off at the bakery.

The search of the bakery went as well as could be expected. While there, the FBI agent asked if Melissa could provide the recipe for the particular bread in question. She unlocked her office, opened the safe and pulled out her recipe card box, made a copy of the card, and handed it to the agent. Just as she suspected, all ingredients in the recipe were confiscated by the cops, along with some baking utensils, while also collecting various swabs of the counters and drawers in the back room. Some poor soul got stuck with dumpster diving in the alley behind the bakery. With the search completed, Cory offered Melissa a ride home. She politely declined. She called her assistant, Maddie, to come to the bakery so they could clean up the mess the cops left behind.

After John David dropped off Melissa, he hightailed it over to the Hawkins' residence. Logan had called him to say that Emily's dad really wanted to speak with Aunt Mel. He had no idea what the man wanted, but after hearing Joey Hawkins attack his sister on the news, he certainly needed to talk to him, too.

Sophie Hawkins was still out running errands. Emily answered the door. She had not expected Logan's father, and only recognized him from family pictures at Melissa's house. John David introduced himself. Joey Hawkins came to the door and stuck out his hand to the other man. They shook hands as they both sized up each other. Immediately, John David took the initiative and asked how the man dared to have his daughter contact Logan to set up a meeting with Melissa after Joey had the audacity to attack her publicly for something she absolutely did not do. Emily's father hung his head in shame for his poor judgment in the matter. He admitted his egregious mistake and apologized. Joey also vowed to apologize to Melissa in person.

Emily chimed in that she knew neither Logan nor his aunt had anything to do with what happened to her grandfather. She added that they desperately needed to find out what happened. She brought out the file folder she discovered in the office earlier that morning. John David read it over thoroughly. Being a speed reader, it didn't take him too long. When finished, he looked up and asked what Joey planned to do with the information. From his viewpoint, it certainly proved Mr. Johnson or someone involved with the deal with the chemical company had motive to kill Mr. Hawkins. "Why haven't you shown this to the cops yet?" he asked. Joey explained that they fully intended to share this with the authorities. Due to his recent bad behavior, he had wanted to apologize to Melissa and Logan first and share the information with them. According to Emily, the aunt and nephew were fairly good at solving mysteries. Perhaps the information would be beneficial as they searched for the truth. Maybe Melissa could ascertain how her bread was poisoned if she had this information. If a comparison could be made between the poison found in the bread and the poison in the illegal weed killer, it would prove Johnson Shipping International had not only motive, but the means to kill Mr. Hawkins.

After making copies of the files, John David took one copy home to Melissa. Joey planned to hand over the originals to the police, but would keep a copy for himself. As John David made to leave the house, he stopped as a thought struck him. He turned to Joey and asked if he could obtain a copy of his father's bank records for the last few months leading up to his death. Puzzled, he questioned why the other man needed it. John David explained that he could audit his father's financial records to determine if he received extra payments from Johnson or some other company that could be viewed as hush money. If they traced any suspicious funds coming into the account, it would lend further credence to the theory that Johnson was somehow involved. If nothing else, someone needed to shed light on the illegal dealings with the chemical company. Being in the financial regulation industry, John David was just the man to make sure that happened. Joey liked the idea and agreed to get the information to him.

Just as Melissa's brother pulled out of the Hawkins' driveway, Sophie returned. Both Joey and his daughter agreed it was best to keep all that had transpired hushed up. When questioned about the unfamiliar car leaving their house, Emily simply explained that Logan's father had stopped by to offer his condolences and to reassure the family that his sister and his son had nothing to do with her grandfather's death. "Well, of course they didn't, sweetie," Sophie replied. "I've been trying to explain that to your knucklehead of a father here. Your grandfather simply died of a heart attack or something like it." Happy to delude herself that Joey would drop the matter now and tell the cops to cease their investigation, she hummed softly as she went back to her bedroom to put away the new clothes she'd just purchased.

John David called Melissa as he drove back towards the bakery. Melissa asked him to meet her at her attorney's office. She had an idea. When he arrived, the two women were already deep in conversation in Janice's tiny office. Melissa repeated what she had already told the attorney about the search of her home and business. John David then filled them in on the information given to him by Joey Hawkins. This mystery was getting more interesting by the minute. Melissa had an idea. If someone analyzed the bread found at the scene against her own recipe, maybe they could discover if someone injected the poison into an actual loaf from her bakery or if someone cooked the poisoned bread themselves, but tried to pass it off as her bread. Of course, it would be best if Melissa could be in on the analysis since she would know exactly what goes into her lemon sage bread and could point out any differences. John

David picked up the phone to dial Joey. Being a bigwig at the State Department and already throwing his weight around with the Kill Devil Hills police, perhaps he could use some influence with the FBI to have the bread thoroughly evaluated. After a brief discussion with Joey, Melissa's brother turned to her with a big smile.

Chapter 15

Having friends in high places certainly helped. By the end of the day, FBI Agent Elijah Young called Melissa. They arranged for her to be present early the next morning as they tested the bread to verify the ingredients corresponded to those she utilized for her own bread. What he failed to mention was that the package had been tested. It was indeed a bag from Melissa's bakery, but there was evidence of tampering with the bag. The interior of the bag showed residue of a completely different type of bread – cranberry orange bread, not lemon sage. Detective Bronson reviewed the receipts from the Kill Devil Delicacies over the last couple months. Mrs. Hawkins had purchased a lot of lemon sage bread for her family. However, she only purchased one loaf of the cranberry orange bread the week of Mr. Hawkins' death.

Melissa arrived early the next morning to help with the bread evaluation. Just in case it was needed, she baked a new loaf of lemon sage bread. She also brought in a loaf from the freezer at the bakery for comparison. In a large box, she brought in all the ingredients. The police already seized her utensils and her large Cuisinart food processor. Shocked to see Melissa entering the precinct, Jason ran over to help her carry her load. Inwardly, Melissa was happy to see him. She realized his boss probably ordered him to stay away from her during the investigation, but it still hurt not to see him every day. After dropping off the things in the forensics lab, Jason squeezed her hand to reassure her. As Agent Young shooed him out of the lab, he mouthed "I love you," to Melissa.

Cory was against having the suspect involved with the testing of the bread and made his thoughts on the matter well known. However, Joey Hawkins had been causing a ruckus in the department. He insisted Melissa be present during the evaluation. Cory and the FBI agent agreed to keep mum on anything else dealing with the case. They had not even let the chief know the FBI was pursuing a judicial order to confiscate the cremains of Mr. Hawkins for testing. Not many police departments were aware of the technology to test human remains after cremation. However, it was something the FBI had invested in. If Mr. Hawkins was indeed poisoned, as they believed, the cremains held the answer.

Melissa observed as the agent analyzed the fresh bread she brought in, as well as the frozen loaf. After some time, the printer spit out a piece of paper showing a breakdown of the ingredients, along with chemical compositions. The list matched the recipe card Melissa had provided. Then the agent ran the same analysis on the bread found with Mr. Hawkins. Agent Young looked perplexed as the report came through. Aside from the addition of the poison in that bread sample, some key ingredients differed. Instead of fresh lemon zest, it contained commercial lemon juice with high fructose corn syrup. The kind found in the plastic lemon-shaped bottles at the grocery store. It also contained a generic brand of dried sage. Melissa only used fresh organic sage grown in her own herb garden at her home. The search conducted the day before had included digging up her herb garden for the sage. The cops had also managed to devastate her basil and oregano crops in the process. Her zesters from both the house and the bakery had also been taken into evidence.

Along with some other ingredients that differed in quantity and quality, the evaluation proved the poisoned bread was not made following Melissa's lemon sage bread recipe. Cory asserted that the test results did not exonerate Melissa, but it raised more questions. He knew that the search of her home and bakery, and even the garbage bins, revealed that Melissa only used fresh ingredients. She was very much a stickler for organic, as well. Whoever baked the poisoned loaf had not taken fresh or organic into consideration at all. As a matter of fact, the person used mostly generic ingredients. Melissa realized it was still an uphill battle to convince Detective Knucklehead she wasn't involved, but this was definitely a good start.

Melissa left the precinct smiling. She didn't stop to speak with Jason, but flashed him a smile on the way out. He knew she was innocent and he knew she wouldn't rest until this mystery was solved. He just wished he could help her more. The grumpy look on Cory's face as he came out of the forensics lab almost made Jason erupt in laughter. The detective admired the younger man's tenacity, but he thought Cory could use a little comeuppance to bring him back down to reality. The realization that his case was falling apart should have given him some fresh perspective, but Jason doubted that highly. However, he was surprised when Agent Young approached him later that afternoon. Along with the chief, the three men met briefly. Without revealing too much information, the agent conceded that he no longer believed Mrs. Maples was involved in Hawkins' death. At this point, there was no evidence to indicate Mr. Hawkins even ate the bread. Yes, the bread was poisoned, but was a bad copy of Mrs. Maples' famous bread.

The FBI agent struggled with presenting the questions, but eventually asked Jason to relay to his girlfriend that they may need her help in catching the bad guy. Someone had gone to an awful lot of trouble to poison Mr. Hawkins. They had the forethought to package the faux bread in the Kill Devil Delicacies packaging, so it was certainly premeditated. However, the agent was confused in that Mr. Hawkins showed no signs of having eaten the bread. Even if he had, based on studies of this particular poison, the result would have appeared as cardiovascular distress. Mr. Hawkins' medical records indicated he had untreated coronary artery disease anyway. To make the call whether the poison killed him or his heart just gave out, the agent wasn't confident they would ever really know. His concern was that Detective Bronson wouldn't just let it go if they couldn't make a definitive connection from the bread to Mr. Hawkins' demise. They agreed that Cory was kind of a like a shark in the water once he smelled blood. The stumbling block for the entire case could be less the case and more the detective.

Relieved that Melissa was no longer really considered a suspect, Jason left the station that night and drove directly to her house. He knew the agent held back some information from him. Jason was fine with that. He was just grateful Agent Young had confided as much as he did with him. He didn't know what would happen next, but he was convinced Melissa would be proven innocent soon.

Chapter 16

Joey Hawkins kept true to his word. Early the next morning, at Melissa's house, he dropped off his parent's financial records over the last few months for John David to analyze. He felt a tinge of regret not telling his own mother about the move, but he knew her to be a blabbermouth and gossip. The last thing he wanted was for this news to get out. Emily tagged along with her father so she could hang out with Logan for a while. With everything going on, they had spent very little time together so far this summer. They had both waited all year for summer's return so they could see each other again. As his father perused the financial documents, Logan took Emily for a long walk along the shore. Joey and Melissa relaxed on the back deck and tried making small talk. The situation was awkward at first, but Melissa's easy-going attitude was contagious. Before he knew it, Joey was actually relaxed for the first time in weeks.

As the young couple returned from their walk, John David called out to Joey to show him what he found. He was an expert at auditing complex financial records and finding irregularities for multi-million dollar companies. Reviewing the Hawkins' bank records had been a piece of cake. William Hawkin's retirement funds had been released to an investment account. John David recognized the particular investment device as one normally utilized to keep funds locked up. It would take a great deal of paperwork for those monies to be available to the account holder or a beneficiary. Joey asked if his mother had direct access to the account, seeing as she was spending money like water and the life insurance policy had not paid out yet. John David suggested that he contact the investment counselor at the bank assigned to the account. However, unless Joey was one of the account holders, the bank could not give out that information.

That wasn't the only peculiar activity regarding the Hawkins' financials though. Starting the date of Mr. Hawkins' sudden retirement, exactly $9,500 was deposited into the account every week. John David explained that if the transactions had been in cash, red flags would have been raised at the amount and frequency. Cash deposits of $10,000 immediately raised red flags to government agencies. He further detailed how there were occasions when the government swooped in and confiscated the 'questionable' funds. Government regulations deemed such financial activities as 'suspicious'. Mostly they utilized the excuse that the funds could be seen as potential evidence related to terrorism or drug dealing. Since the amount was under $10,000 and transferred electronically, the transactions had stayed just under the radar.

Joey Hawkins was floored. According to the financial records in front of him, his parents' bank account had exponentially increased over the last few weeks. William and Sophie Hawkins had always been upper-middle class, although his mother always acted as if they were even beyond that. Now, his mom sat on a mountain of money. She could certainly afford to live out the lifestyle she desired with that much coming in every week.

"Do the records show where the money came from?" Joey asked. Shaking his head, John David informed him that the only way to find out would be to contact the bank. However, a warrant would be needed for the information, unless Sophie Hawkins gave her express permission to the bank. "Well, that's highly unlikely," Joey muttered.

The two men discussed their options, but the situation was grim. They could provide the information to the police for them to pursue the issue. However, Mrs. Hawkins could protest since her son took the information without her approval or knowledge. That could lead to Joey and John David ending up in the slammer.

Having returned early from their walk, Logan and Emily overheard most of their conversation. Logan suggested that if the poison was traced back to Johnson's holding company then couldn't the police obtain a warrant for the company's financial records. It seemed to make sense that the money came from Johnson's company since the influx began at the time of Mr. Hawkins' retirement. However, the young man mused why the money kept coming in after the man's death. Melissa piped in with the information Ronnie had given her about Sophie Hawkins showing up at the company shortly after her husband's abrupt retirement announcement. This was the first Joey heard about the encounter. The dismay was evident on his face. He realized that perhaps it was time someone questioned his mother.

Joey made a quick call to the police department. He left out the information about his parents' finances and his suspicion that the funds came from Johnson's company, perhaps as a bribe to keep his dad silent. Using his authoritative, stern voice as intimidation, he demanded that the police question his father's employer about his sudden retirement. The chief quickly assured him that the department agreed questioning Mr. Johnson was an excellent idea. "Actually," the chief confided, "it is being done as we speak." Joey remarked that he was happy to hear that news. Before ending the call, he coyly asked if the department needed his mother to come in to give her statement. "It's funny that you ask, Mr. Hawkins. We planned to call your mother in later this afternoon for just that purpose." Joey was impressed. Maybe the Kill Devil Hill police department knew what it was doing after all.

After thanking John David and Melissa for their help, Joey returned home to encourage his mother to go to the precinct and tell the cops everything she knew about Dad's sudden retirement. He knew she would be livid about the situation. He just wanted to make her understand it was the only way to find out if Dad had been murdered. The police needed to cover all angles. If Mr. Johnson had anything to do with his father's death, perhaps Mom knew more than she thought she did. Perhaps she had key information the police needed to crack the case. If she didn't cooperate, he intended to bring out the papers Emily found in the file cabinet that showed his father's knowledge of Johnson's illicit dealings with the chemical company.

Joey didn't really want Emily around the house. He fully expected his mother to make a scene about being called into the police station. The chief assured him that, if needed, they could send a patrol car to pick her up. He hoped it didn't come to that.

Logan offered to take Emily back to the beach for a surf lesson to keep her mind otherwise occupied. The young woman smiled at her father with an unspoken "Please". He readily agreed. The two teens grabbed Logan's surf board and ran out the door. Melissa smiled at the retreating backs of the young couple. Deciding she had neglected her business long enough, she called Maddie at the bakery to let her know she would be arriving there in a little while.

Chapter 17

Joey was right to worry. By the time he arrived home the police had already called. Sophie Hawkins was in a complete meltdown. He found her in the living room scooping ashes from the fireplace into the urn that contained William Hawkins' cremains. Completely aghast, he ran over to stop her. "Mother, what are you doing?" he asked in shock. She stared blankly back at him. After a few moments, she appeared to gather her wits about her again. Smiling, she confessed what she was doing looked a bit odd, but it was all for the best. Not able to comprehend her logic and sick of dealing with her nonsense, Joey's anger burst forth. How dare she fill his father's urn with soot and ash!

Sophie Hawkins had never in her life been on the wrong side of her son's temper. So upset at the tone of his voice, she started trembling. He again asked what she was doing. His face red with anger. In a shaken voice, she admitted that the cops had called earlier. They wanted her for questioning. "They want to question ME!" she said almost hysterically. "Me! I'm the blasted widow, not a suspect! How dare they tell me that I have to come to the police station! I've done nothing wrong!"

Still not understanding her actions, Joey tried again. The look that crossed Sophie's face made a shiver run down his spine. He could almost see her mind working to come up with a suitable answer as a smile crept across her features. "Don't you see, honey? The cops…they performed autopsies on dead seagulls just so they would have an excuse to defile your father's remains. That's why I had him cremated. You see, I knew even then that the cops would insist your poor father didn't die of natural causes. They just have to have someone to blame for everything. Look what they did to that poor baker woman last summer." She leaned in close to whisper, "The cops want me to bring in your father's cremains for testing. Can you believe that? Have you ever heard of such a thing? Well, I wouldn't let them defile your father's body by performing an autopsy. I'm surely not going to allow them to defile his cremains."

The poor man was so shaken and appalled by her words that he fell to his knees. Sophie knelt beside her son while tenderly petting the top of his head as if he were still a small child. "Don't worry, sweetheart. I already moved William's ashes to a different container. The cops won't know what to make of the ashes and will have to drop the whole thing," she soothed.

Gathering his strength back, Joey grabbed his mother's wrist. "Show me where Dad's cremains are now!" he ordered. He couldn't understand if his mom had lost complete touch with reality or was just so concerned about losing her newfound wealth that she would actively withhold evidence that could prove Johnson poisoned his father. Did she really only care about the money? Why did his mother not desire justice for her husband? After recovering the cremains from a plastic container in the laundry room, Joey drove his mother and the cremains to the police station.

They entered the precinct to the sound of loud voices emanating from the chief's office. Mr. Johnson's lawyer, Peter Andrews, was in full lambasting mode as he insisted his client be released immediately. Everyone else in the department stood frozen in place as they listened to the heated exchange. Detective Bronson hurried over to the Hawkins family. He thanked Mrs. Hawkins for coming in and for bringing in her husband's cremains. She reluctantly handed over the plastic container. Although confused why the cremains were now housed in plastic instead of the expensive bronze memorial urn from the funeral home, Cory handed the container off to a uniformed officer for cataloging. The detective then led the widow and her son to an empty conference room down the hall. As Sophie Hawkins passed the chief's office window, Peter Andrews turned around just in time to lock eyes with her. Joey noticed as a frightened look came over his mother's face as she stumbled a step before continuing to follow the detective. By the time they reached the other room, she fully recovered herself with no signs of further distress.

Back in the chief's office, the FBI agent also noted the exchange between the lawyer and Mrs. Hawkins. Mr. Andrews' confrontational demeanor changed. After a moment or two, he requested that he be allowed to talk with his client in private for a few minutes. Neither the chief nor Agent Young understood the alteration. They hoped it meant someone was about to come clean and this whole mystery would be solved. Knowing Mr. Johnson, the chief was not optimistic.

The attorney and Mr. Johnson spoke in hushed tones while the others waited outside the office. At his desk a few yards away, Jason would have given anything to be a fly on the wall in that room right then. It didn't take long for the attorney to stick his head out the office door to reconvene the meeting. As Chief Monroe and the FBI agent re-entered the room, Mr. Johnson held his head high with a stern, but determined look. The chief knew that whatever information the tycoon was about to give them came at a huge price. Mr. Andrews began the conversation by requesting, no demanding, full immunity be given to his client. "Full immunity from what exactly?" Agent Young asked. However, Chief Monroe interjected that only the district attorney's office had the authority to make deals. Peter Andrews corrected the chief. For the information that his client could deliver would require a higher level of authority, such as only the FBI or the Department of Justice wielded. The chief groaned. This negotiation was going to take a long time.

Chapter 18

The precinct waited on pins and needles to find out what was going on in Chief Monroe's office. Mrs. Hawkins became more and more agitated as she waited in the conference room down the hall. She picked her fingernails and shifted uncomfortably in her seat. It seemed everything had reached a standstill. It was so quiet in the department that a number of people jumped when the silence was penetrated by the shrill ring of the phone on Detective Payne's desk.

Melissa was on the line and in a panic. She explained that she was on her way to the emergency room with Emily. Although she didn't know the specifics, she told him that the two teenagers had gone back to the Hawkins' residence. At some point, Emily started experiencing severe heart palpitations. Logan called his aunt for advice. Her assistant, Maddie, drove her over to the house to check on the girl. Minutes before her arrival, Emily passed out. Thankfully, Logan knew enough to call 911 first. The ambulance pulled up just as Melissa got out of Maddie's car. She didn't know anything about the girl's condition, but needed Jason to track down Emily's father. He heard the fear in her voice. He wished more than anything he was there to put his arms around her to reassure her. He promised to bring Joey to the hospital himself.

Jason burst into the conference room where Joey sat trying to reason with his mother to simply tell the cops everything so they could get justice for his father. The detective didn't know how to put the news into soothing words, so he blurted out that Emily was on her way to the hospital. Both Joey and Sophie Hawkins jumped up. Jason offered to take them both over in his own car. Shaken, they accepted. On the way out, Jason informed his partner about Emily's plight.

After they left the precinct, Cory rushed back to the forensics laboratory. He requested that they put a rush on the cremains testing before Mrs. Hawkins changed her mind and demanded them back. Almost as an afterthought, he decided to take one of the technicians with him to the hospital. Before leaving, he knocked on the chief's door. Cory requested that he speak with Agent Young for a moment. He advised the agent of what have transpired with the victim's granddaughter. With a quizzical look, the agent nodded. The two had one last trick up their sleeves. They already had search warrants for the Johnson International Shipping offices, as well as for the Hawkins' residence. They agreed that the best time to act on it was when the widow was not at home and Mr. Johnson and his attorney were otherwise occupied. Now was the perfect time. While Agent Young rounded up a group of uniformed officers and a couple of forensic lab technicians, Detective Bronson headed over to the hospital.

When Jason arrived at the hospital with Joey and Sophie, Emily had been taken back to radiology for a heart scan. Melissa and Logan waited anxiously outside the secured doors to the emergency room. Since they were not relatives, the staff would not allow them to go back with the young girl and would not give updates on her condition. They only knew that Emily had been resuscitated in the ambulance on the way to the hospital. She was breathing on her own, which was an excellent sign. Joey marched up to the reception desk to demand he be permitted to see his daughter. A nurse escorted him back.

Emily had just been returned to the emergency room cubicle from radiology. Seeing his daughter connected by various wires and tubes to machines monitoring her vital signs made tears spring to Joey's eyes. He loved his daughter with his whole heart and never wanted to see her in such a sad state. Her skin was a ghastly pale shade with dark circles under her eyes. He realized that he had been in such a rush that he had not even called her mother. Joey hoped his own mother had the sense to call her for him. He doubted it though. Sophie had been frantic on her way over to the hospital.

He walked softly over to a small metal chair beside the bed. Emily appeared to sleep. He took her hand and pressed it to his lips. As tears flowed down his face, he promised the moon and the stars if only she'd just wake up and be healthy again. She stirred a little, but could barely open her eyes. Instead, she squeezed his hand as if to let him know she was going to be okay.

Jason was surprised when his partner entered the small waiting area outside the emergency room, followed by a lab technician from the department. Cory politely asked about Emily's condition, then requested to speak with Jason privately. Despite the fact he was not allowed to work the case due to his affiliation with Melissa, Cory filled Jason in on the searches that were being conducted. He wanted Jason's assistance with getting Joey Hawkins to give them permission to take a blood sample from his daughter. The older detective began to see where his partner was going with the new direction of the investigation. He agreed, but needed to speak with Joey when he was away from his mother.

An hour went by agonizingly slow as they waited for word of Emily's condition. Sophie peppered Logan with questions about what Emily had been doing prior to falling ill. He explained that they returned from the surfing lesson to find no one home. Emily was hungry for something sweet so she offered to make a dessert for them. Although not a fancy pastry chef like his aunt, she promised she could make crazy good smoothies. He didn't even have a chance to taste it. Almost immediately after testing a spoonful herself before serving it, Emily suddenly felt very ill and grasped her chest in pain. The poor girl's grandmother was visibly upset so Melissa came over to wrap an arm around the woman's shoulders to comfort her.

Finally, Joey came out to let them know she was being moved to the intensive care unit (ICU) for observation. The doctors still did not know what caused Emily's heart palpitations. Her condition was stabilized for the time being, but they couldn't promise there would not be a recurrence. At this point, they were puzzled but optimistic the tests performed would reveal the true culprit so they could make a proper diagnosis.

Sophie interrupted her son. "What did the doctors say about heart palpitations? She's just a young girl.

Why would she experience that?" she asked with a shaky voice. Joey explained that something caused Emily's otherwise normal heart to beat extremely fast and then slow to almost a standstill before racing again. She experienced agonizing pain, quite similar to a heart attack. However, she was sedated and resting comfortably now.

The grandmother let out a wail of sorrow. She began rocking back and forth muttering, "It's all my fault! It's all my fault!" Over and over again she repeated the words as her voice grew louder each time. Everyone stood back in silent shock as they tried to make sense of the manic woman before them. Cory and Jason exchanged glances. They knew one of them needed to get Mrs. Hawkins to elaborate on what exactly was her fault.

As the truth began to dawn on Joey, he knelt beside his mother. Closing his eyes, he willed himself to speak the awful question that needed to be asked. "Mother," he began, "what did you do?"

Chapter 19

As rays of sunshine penetrated the flimsy shades of her hospital room, Emily opened her eyes. Still incredibly fatigued, she felt much better. She recalled being brought into the hospital and being poked and prodded. She looked over to find her father fast asleep in an oversized recliner near the window. Clearing her throat, she attempted to wake him. Joey bolted upright at the noise. He quickly realized his daughter made the noise and her eyes were open again. Saying a silent prayer of thanks, he rushed to her bedside.

With the help of Emily's grandmother, the doctors were able to discover the source of the young woman's ailment and treat it. A transfusion had been required to flush the poison out of Emily's bloodstream. Apparently, when she fixed the smoothies she used the same food processor to chop up her berries and kale that Sophie used to mix the ingredients of her version of Melissa's lemon sage bread. Despite cleaning all the utensils, a small trace of the poison remained stuck on the processor's blades.

The doctors admitted that if they waited for the lab results, Emily would have survived, but there could have been long-term damage to her heart. Mrs. Hawkins coming forward so quickly with the suggestion it was poison and the particular type of poison made their jobs a lot easier. Joey was grateful his daughter's life and health would be spared, but he was furious with his mother. He thought Emily still too frail to hear the entire truth. When she was stronger he would explain the situation fully.

Last night's revelations rocked Joey to his core. It's not every day you hear your own mother confess to planning to murder your father. The question still remained whether William Hawkins died of the poison or whether he died of a heart attack. The doctors explained that because Emily had a strong healthy heart, the poison wasn't fatal. However, his father had been known to have coronary artery disease. Even the slightest contact with the poison could've triggered a cardiac episode. He really wished he'd intervened earlier, before his father's body was cremated.

The police jumped into action when Sophie confessed. Apparently, there was already some suspicion. The search of the Hawkins' home uncovered several items that were now in police custody – the food processor, bottled lemon juice, commercial (non-organic) dried sage, and a small pill bottle in Sophie's bathroom medicine cabinet containing a powdery substance. Along with the financial records Joey turned over to the police and his father's files on the illegal dealings between Johnson Shipping International and the chemical holding company, the confession was enough to warrant the arrest of Mrs. Sophie Hawkins for at least the attempted murder of Mr. Williams Hawkins.

Sadly, the woman's excuse was simply that she wanted more money to live the life she thought she deserved. She felt her husband's retirement funds were insufficient to keep her in the lap of luxury. The poor woman cried as she explained that the couple had long ago lost 'that loving feeling' and she had started to see William as simply a means to obtain the things she wanted. The extra money coming in from Johnson had been the result of her blackmailing the company with William's files on the illicit dealings with the weed killer company. With the dirty money and her husband's hefty life insurance policy to supplement his retirement account, she fully intended to live the good life for the rest of her days.

As for Mr. Johnson, the FBI decided to not authorize an immunity deal for information against Mrs. Hawkins. They had enough evidence to convict her for her husband's death. They also now had enough information from Mr. Hawkins' files to pursue an intensive investigation against Johnson for corporate misdealing and regulatory violations. Mrs. Hawkins' own testimony revealed the company forced her husband out of his job when he wouldn't sweep the chemical company deal under the proverbial rug for them.

In her interview with Detective Bronson and Agent Young, Sophie admitted that the company's lawyer advised her how to deal with questions regarding the monetary inflow, as well as how to handle any questions after her husband's demise. Although she had not informed the lawyer of the use of the poison she found amongst her husband's things from the office, it was Peter Andrews that recommended Mr. Hawkins be cremated. This made the attorney an accessory to attempted murder.

Back at the precinct, Jason and Cory worked all night. They had not even been home to shower and change clothes when a forensics technician called them into the lab. Although, the Kill Devil Hills police department had never tested cremains for poisons or drugs, the FBI agent had provided them with the proper equipment and instructions to perform the tests. The report clearly stated that no poison was found in Mr. Hawkins' ashes. If he ingested the poison, even the slightest amount, it should've shown in the test results. Mr. William Hawkins had not died of nefarious causes. His wife may have intended to poison him, but in the end it was his own faulty ticker that just gave out.

Chapter 20

Another summer in Kill Devil Hills flew by too fast
for the young man. It had been quite another season
of mystery and adventure. "Thankfully," he thought,
"all's well that ends well". Emily recovered quickly
from her exposure to the poison. However, she had
yet to heal from the emotional scars after she learned
her grandmother had intended to poison her
grandfather. The fact that he did indeed die of
natural causes failed to alleviate the pain. Her family
and friends, especially Logan, worked hard all
summer to help her heal physically and emotionally.

At first Logan feared that Emily would no longer
stay in the small seaside town during the summer
since her grandmother was locked up. However,
Joey Hawkins surprised everyone, including
himself, when he decided that the family needed
more quality time together. What better place to do
that than to take off from his strenuous job during
the summer and relax at the beach? Emily was
overjoyed. Her mother and older brother were
shocked! The family had never taken an extended
vacation together. Dad always worked. For years he
reasoned that his job took them to exotic places so
that substituted for real vacations. The move had

proven highly beneficial to Emily's well-being, as well as the rest of the family. By the end of the summer the family agreed that every summer should be spent together in Kill Devil Hills, NC. This, of course, made Logan Jones very happy.

The events of early summer had other long-lasting effects for the Jones family. Logan expected his dad to rush back to Charlotte, NC to his career. Instead, John David stuck around for another week to spend some much needed quality time with his son. They agreed Logan should stay with his aunt the rest of the summer, as usual. However, some things changed. Every other weekend throughout the summer John David and his wife drove out to visit their son. The couple even took an unheard of two week vacation in July to celebrate Logan's birthday.

Melissa didn't mind one bit having all the extra people staying with her in the small bungalow home. It gave her a chance to reconnect with her brother. Besides, witnessing the growing bond between John David and his son melted her heart. It was long overdue. However, her attempts to teach her sister-in-law to bake Logan's favorite dessert – actually to teach her to bake anything – tried even Melissa's most patient soul.

As the summer drew to a close, Melissa hosted a picnic at the beach for the entire Jones and Hawkins families, as well as close friends. Tanner even showed up with a Yeti cooler full of water bottles and sodas, in lieu of his usual disguised beer cans. For the first time in their acquaintance, Janice walked up in shorts and a tank top instead of her modest business suits and sensible heels. However, she did have an interesting accessory on her arm – a certain young detective by the name of Cory Bronson. Melissa shook her head. How those two ever got together was beyond her comprehension. The two appeared very happy though. Cory had immediately and profusely apologized to Melissa at the end of the investigation of Mr. Hawkins' death. At one point, his continuous requests for forgiveness became downright comical.

Melissa watched as Logan and Emily strolled hand in hand down the beach. She was so grateful that the two youngsters managed to not only maintain their friendship throughout the ordeal, but had become even closer. Just then, an arm reached around Melissa's waist. She leaned back into Jason's strong, broad chest. Closing her eyes, she felt peaceful. With the end of summer, things around Kill Devil Hills would slow down to their normal routine. She knew she would miss having her family around the nine long months until next summer. However, this time she realized with satisfaction that her nephew no longer faced those months feeling alone and ignored by his parents. From now on, the young man would experience all the love and attention a strong family had to offer. Despite the crazy circumstances that brought them to this place, the result was indeed worth all the trouble. Witnessing the renewed bond between father and son, Melissa sighed. This was a true family. She couldn't have been any happier.

Your Free Gift

I wanted to show my appreciation for supporting my work so I've put together a Bonus Chapter for you.

Just visit:

http://outerbanks2_freegift.gr8.com

Thanks!
Phoebe T. Eggli

Timber Publishing

Sample Chapter from Book 3 of the Outer Banks Baker Mystery Series

A Time to Live and a Thyme to Die

Chapter 1

For once Melissa Maples' summer started out relatively uneventful. The last two summers had been chalk full of mystery and mayhem from the get-go. Two years ago, she walked into her own bakery with her beloved nephew Logan to discover the dead body of a rival baker. One year ago, Logan found the dead body of his girlfriend's grandfather on his first day of fishing at Oregon Inlet. Both deaths tied back to her and the bakery somehow and they spent the early part of both summers fighting to prove their innocence in both events.

This summer started out peaceful, for the most part. At least no dead bodies, so for Melissa, that was a huge plus in her book. Logan was back for his annual visit. Another visitor was in town this year though. Kristina Payne, Jason Payne's daughter, was staying with her dad for the summer before heading off to the University of North Carolina (UNC) – Wilmington in the fall. She surprised her dad by showing up at his house the first day of summer vacation. Apparently, she hitchhiked to town from Elizabeth City. That wasn't the only surprise for her father. Krissy sported an entirely new look Jason didn't necessarily approve of, but knew enough to realize there was nothing to be accomplished by yelling at an eighteen year old woman about her blue hair and nose piercing. Melissa hoped to forge a relationship with her boyfriend's daughter. It felt so strange to use the term "boyfriend" when she was 46 years old, but it was appropriate. However, the young woman had other ideas completely that did not align with the hopes of Melissa and Jason.

Kristina, or Krissy as she preferred to be called, was a troubled girl on the verge of womanhood. Despite the recent remarriage of her mother, she was not thrilled that dear old dad was seriously dating someone. Every effort to befriend the girl had been outright rebuffed. When Melissa offered her a job at the bakery to earn some money for college, Krissy rudely refused. Not to be deterred, Melissa arranged for her friend Cheryl to hire the girl at her own soup, salad, and sandwich shop across the street from the Kill Devil Delicacies bakery. Krissy never knew her father's girlfriend engineered the job opening, and that was perfectly fine with Melissa.

They tried biweekly dinners at Melissa's house, too. Although Logan and Jason enjoyed Mel's culinary expertise, Krissy made sure to let everyone know her disdain for anything deemed non-traditional. The middle-aged widow spent her life in the kitchen as a pastry chef. She was renowned for her artisan breads and even won the Outer Banks Regional Bake-Off two years ago. Gourmet French meals were also a specialty of hers. Of course, Logan preferred hamburgers and French fries like any teenager but after several summers with Aunt Mel, he found he started to enjoy the gourmet meals just as much. Krissy, however, would sit at the table without saying a word and not touching her food. After dinner, she would excuse herself and run to the closest fast food chain, as evidenced by the pile-up of wrappers in the passenger side of her father's truck. Melissa tried her hand at more traditional fare in an effort to appease the young woman, but nothing she did or cooked seemed to be satisfactory. Still, she held out hope that by the end of the summer she and Krissy could become friends.

Now in the middle of June, the group settled into a somewhat comfortable pattern of everyday life. Logan helped Melissa out at the bakery in the mornings and then spent his afternoons with his girlfriend, Emily once she arrived back in town with her family. The poor kid tried to befriend Krissy too, but the young woman didn't seem interested in making new friends, especially with anyone who thought Melissa was the best. Logan adored his aunt and could not tolerate Krissy's snide remarks under her breath about her. Emily really didn't appreciate the attitude Jason's daughter exuded towards a family she had grown to love and respect. However, everyone was determined to try their best for Jason's sake.

Life had been more disruptive over the last week. Krissy's no-good boyfriend, Derek McCallie, arrived in town. Needless to say, Jason was not thrilled. The boy reeked of trouble. A phone call to his ex-wife revealed the young man was not the epitome of what a nice southern young man should be, what with being kicked out of school in the middle of his senior year along with a growing arrest record. Krissy claimed he turned his life around complete with passing his GED exam and a new job with a moving company in town. Ever a sucker for a story of a reformed young person, Jason caved and didn't ban Krissy from seeing Derek. Melissa had a bad feeling he would soon regret that decision.

Melissa's thoughts often returned to how to better her own relationship with Krissy. After dating Jason for almost two years, she considered her present and future to be with him. It would be nice to have his daughter's blessing. She pondered that very issue as she mixed up a few more recipes to refrigerate overnight in the back room of her bakery. Logan already left to join Emily's family for an early dinner and Jason was resting up for the night shift with his partner, Cory Bronson.

With her hands and arms covered in sweet-smelling flour she mixed and kneaded while her mind drifted to the latest story from her friend Cheryl about the misadventures of employing Jason's daughter in her soup and salad shop – Cheryl's Seaside Sundries. Apparently, the blue hair and nose piercing weren't the only adornments Krissy had obtained. Cheryl called earlier to say she saw a peek-a-boo tattoo in the small of her back as the girl bent over to pick up something that spilled on the floor. Her straight-laced cop father would not be impressed. Melissa had no plans to tell him either. Cheryl tried to figure out what the tattoo was, but when she leaned to get a closer look she accidently knocked over a container of salad on top of the poor girl's head. Melissa would've paid money to see that. According to Cheryl, it was quite humorous to see the horrified look on Krissy's face as spinach and walnuts clumped in her blue hair and balsamic vinaigrette dripped down her forehead and off her nose. Clearly, the young woman didn't appreciate the laughter that Cheryl could not contain.

Krissy ran off in a huff to change clothes with a few select words muttered under her breath. She commandeered her father's truck during her stay.

Melissa heard the tires squeal as the young woman sped away. Cheryl called her immediately after the episode. Her friend could barely get the story out in between fits of laughter.

After putting away the pans of dough in the large refrigerator, Melissa came out to the front of her bakery. Her assistant, Maddie, had everything well in hand. It was an unusually quiet afternoon in the bakery for the middle of the tourist season. Pouring herself another cup of coffee, Melissa sat down for a few moments to rest while absentmindedly listening to the local North Carolina coast news on a small television in the corner of the bakery reception area. A young woman with too much red lipstick reported from the local hospital where there had been several cases of a strange nature. The symptoms were all similar – extreme fatigue, vomiting, losing consciousness – but the doctors were stumped. Over twenty new patients had been admitted to the hospital just that day with fifteen admitted overnight. "Oh dear," Maddie said softly, "Just what we need to scare off the tourists – a friggin' epidemic!" At that, Melissa rolled her eyes a little. Maddie always made a mountain out of a mole hill. She suspected the same here.

As Melissa got back up to check on some rolls in the oven, she saw Jason's truck drive by way too fast for the small street. "Krissy's back," she thought to herself. She halted in her tracks as she heard the truck's brakes screech to an abrupt stop. A moment later, the quiet afternoon air was pierced with a horrifying scream. Without thinking, Melissa ran out the front door to the alleyway leading from the main street behind Cheryl's shop. She found Krissy on her knees in front of the truck, crying and screaming uncontrollably. Running over to the distraught teenager, Melissa put her arms around her asking if she was alright. Peering over her shoulder, she saw a horrific sight. Apparently, the truck had just missed slamming into poor elderly Mrs. Burnside whose body was lying in the middle of the back alley behind Cheryl's shop where she usually strolled to and from the shop and her home a couple blocks away.

The girl's screams continued, as Melissa yelled for someone to call 9-1-1 and she attempted to remove Krissy from the alley. Cheryl came out and led Krissy away as Melissa checked the woman's vital signs. Mrs. Ethel Burnside, an 82 year old sweet lady who frequented the bakery and Cheryl's shop, was unresponsive in a puddle of her own vomit. An ambulance was called immediately, but it was too late. The sweet woman was pronounced dead at the scene. The quaint seaside town of Kill Devil Hills, NC had its first casualty of the summer and a new mystery was born.

Recipes:

Lemon Sage Bread

Ingredients:

> 4 Cups Flour
> 2 ¼ Cups Water
> 2 tsp Salt
> ¼ tsp Dry Active Yeast
> 2 Tbsp. Fresh Sage Chopped Finely or 1 Tbsp. Dry Sage Flakes
> 2 Tbsp. Lemon Zest
> Cornmeal - Sprinkled in the Dutch oven – not mixed in dry the ingredients

Instructions:

Mix flour, salt and yeast in a large mixing bowl. If using Dry Sage Flakes then mix them in the dry ingredients. Or if you're using Fresh Sage then mix it with the water and allow it to soak in the water for at least 5 minutes to allow the flavor to spread through the water. Then pour and mix the wet ingredients into the dry ingredients. Stir until ingredients are well mixed. Dough may seem extra moist, which is perfectly normal. Then cover the bowl and allow to sit at room temperature for 12-18 hours.

Preheat the oven to 500°F with a cast iron Dutch oven or Le Creuset style enameled pot in the oven preheating as well. Once the oven and Dutch oven has been preheated, pull the Dutch oven out of the oven and remove the lid. Then sprinkle some cornmeal in the bottom of the Dutch oven. On a lightly floured surface pour out the dough, form into a ball, and place the dough ball inside the Dutch oven. Replace the Dutch oven lid and place the Dutch oven in the oven. Bake for 30 minutes, then remove the lid and continue to bake for 8-15 minutes, depending on how brown you want the crust to be.

Note: If you don't have 12-18 hours to allow the dough to rest, you may increase the amount of yeast to 1 tsp and only wait 6 hours before baking the dough. However, the longer you wait, the more sourdough-like the bread will be.

The trick to this bread is allowing it to rest for the 12-18 hours and its high moisture content, which turns to steam while being baked with the lid on the Dutch oven. Once we remove the Dutch oven lid, then we begin to bake the outside for a nice crispy crust!

Italian Herb Bread

Ingredients:

>4 Cups Flour
>2 ¼ Cups Water
>2 tsp Salt
>¼ tsp Dry Active Yeast
>2 Tbsp. Herbes of Provence (Victoria Taylor's
>Seasonings is the best!)
>Cornmeal - Sprinkled in the Dutch oven – not
>mixed in dry the ingredients

Instructions:

Mix flour, salt and yeast and Herbes of Provence
Seasoning in a large mixing bowl. Then add the
water to the dry ingredients. Stir until ingredients are
well mixed. Dough may seem extra moist, which is
perfectly normal. Then cover the bowl and allow to
sit at room temperature for 12-18 hours.

Preheat the oven to 500°F with a cast iron Dutch oven
or Le Creuset style enameled pot in the oven
preheating as well. Once the oven and Dutch oven
has been preheated, pull the Dutch oven out of the
oven and remove the lid. Then sprinkle some
cornmeal in the bottom of the Dutch oven. On a
lightly floured surface pour out the dough, form into a
ball, and place inside of the Dutch oven. Replace the

Dutch oven lid and place the Dutch oven in the oven. Bake for 30 minutes, then remove the lid and continue to bake for 8-15 minutes, depending on how brown you want the crust to be.

Note: If you don't have 12-18 hours to allow the dough to rest, you may increase the amount of yeast to 1 tsp and only wait 6 hours before baking the dough. However, the longer you wait, the more sourdough-like the bread will be.

The trick to this bread is allowing it to rest for the 12-18 hours and its high moisture content, which turns to steam while being baked with the lid on the Dutch oven. Once we remove the Dutch oven lid, then we begin to bake the outside for a nice crispy crust!

This bread naturally pairs with Italian dishes, but I honestly can say that it's well received with almost any fare!

Maddie's Blueberry Cheesecake Muffins

Ingredients:

- 3 Cups Flour
- 1 Cup Sugar
- 4 tsp Baking Powder
- ¼ tsp Salt
- 8oz. Cream Cheese (at room temperature)
- 2 Eggs
- 1 Cup Milk
- 1 tsp. Vanilla extract
- ½ Cup Butter (melted and cooled)
- 1/8 Cup Brown Cane Sugar
- 1/8 Cup Brown Sugar
- ½ tsp Cinnamon

Instructions:

Sift flour, sugar, baking powder and salt into large mixing bowl. In another bowl/mixer beat the cream cheese and eggs until smooth and then add milk, vanilla, and the melted butter, mixing thoroughly. Now add the flour mixture to the cream cheese mixture and mix thoroughly. Now gently fold in the blueberries. Preheat the oven to 400°F. Now spoon the mixture into 12 muffin liners inside of a muffin pan. In another small bowl combine the cane sugar, brown sugar and cinnamon and mix well. Then sprinkle the cinnamon sugar mixture generously on the tops of the muffin mixture in each muffin liner. Bake for 20-25 minutes or until the muffins are firm and beginning to brown.

Ideally, serve them with butter while still warm.

You may want to share them with the local detective. You never know when you might need a friend at the police department!

Also by Phoebe T. Eggli

Book 1 of the Outer Banks Baker Mystery Series

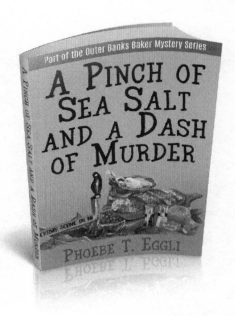

First Published, 2015

Timber Publishing
Oakley, UT 84055
www.timberpublishing.com

Made in the USA
San Bernardino, CA
07 December 2015